UNDER LOCK AND KEY

A WATER WITCH COZY MYSTERY - BOOK ONE

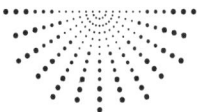

SAM SHORT

WWW.SAMSHORTAUTHOR.COM

Copyright © 2017 by Sam Short

All rights reserved.

No part of this book may be reproduced in any form or by any electronic or mechanical means, including information storage and retrieval systems, without written permission from the author, except for the use of brief quotations in a book review.

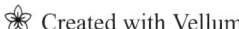 Created with Vellum

For Katie.
My love. My life. My all.

ALSO BY SAM SHORT

Four and Twenty Blackbirds

An Eye For An Eye

A Meeting Of Minds

CHAPTER ONE

"*I*'ll stick this onion so far up your backside, that your breath will smell like a Frenchman's!"

Sacré Bleu! That's not what I expected to hear just as I was about to take a big gulp of wine — or a little sip in my case — naturally. It's lucky that I hadn't managed to get any wine in my mouth — it would have been spluttered all over my clothes, and I knew from bitter experience that elderberry wine does not come out of a white summer dress.

The berries had been picked under a full moon, and the glass which contained the crimson liquid brushed my lips enticingly as the woman's voice echoed around the clearing. I took a last sniff of the fruity aromas and reluctantly placed the glass next to a pot of herbs on the flat roof of my boat.

"I'd better go and have a look," I said to Rosie, who was pacing on the roof behind me, nagging me for her evening meal. "It sounds like somebody's got a bee in their bonnet!"

It's sometimes lonely on a boat, and I unashamedly used Rosie as a surrogate person to talk to. Anyway, I wasn't one of those people who thought speaking to animals was crazy. In fact, some of my most memorable conservations had been with Rosie. One sided as they were.

The cat gave me a look that I interpreted as a final demand, and mewled pleadingly, her black tail swinging in annoyance. "It's not time yet," I said. "Catch a rat if you're that hungry, I'm sure there are plenty along the canal bank."

Rosie looked at me with the disdain I deserved. She would chase rats off the boat, but kill them she would not — and eat them? No chance. I put it down to her being a pacifist, but my friends insisted she was just bone idle and a fussy eater. Maybe it was a mix of both. Either way, my boat was free of vermin, and I was never treated to the macabre gift-giving habits of other people's cats.

I clambered off the roof and stood on the bow deck of the *Water Witch* as the shouting female launched her next verbal barrage, this time a little less xenophobic. Or was it racist? I'd not spoken to Granny for sixteen weeks, so my knowledge of politically correct buzzwords was meagre to say the least. She'd soon jog my memory when I got around to visiting her. "You're an awful man, Sam!" the woman shouted. "A greedy man who should know better! You grew up here in Wickford, how could you do this to us?"

I deduced that the shouting was coming from the shared allotment gardens, which were at the top of one of the three footpaths that led up the hill from my secluded mooring. The woman's threat of using an onion as a highly intrusive weapon strengthened that theory.

The female voice wasn't recognisable, but I guessed who the person she was shouting at was — Sam Hedgewick, local businessman, and owner of the football pitch sized piece of land that was the allotments.

The shouting continued as I stepped ashore onto the strip of stonework which separated my boat from the grass, and skirted the mooring, reminding myself that I'd have to thank whoever it was from the hotel who'd mowed the grass for me. I'd been away for four months, taking my floating witchcraft shop on its first business trip along the canals and rivers of England, and it was nice to come home to freshly cut grass.

The Poacher's Pocket Hotel, hidden by trees on the hill above me, owned the mooring spot I leased, and I could access the hotel's beer garden using the second of the three footpaths. The final path gave me access to the town of Wickford which was a short walk away, and emerged on Bridge Street, near the *Firkin Gherkin* greengrocers.

The hotel had once offered canal trips, and the two picnic benches the customers had used while waiting for the boat, were still there, a few feet from the water's edge. The potted plants I'd left to fend for themselves still looked healthy, and the water and electricity supplies, housed in a green metal box, were the cherry on top of the cake. There'd be no more worrying about the boat's batteries going flat, or having to cruise a few miles to fill up my water tank — until I took my shop on its next trip at least. It was good to be home.

I'd been strangely lucky to have been offered the lease. When the hotel stopped offering boat trips, wealthy people had queued up to buy the unique mooring, but after a visit from my grandmother the hotel owners had offered me the chance to lease it — for a surprisingly affordable monthly fee.

I was convinced that magic had been involved, despite my grandmother's vehement denial. She vehemently denied everything she was accused of though, including the infamous incident of Farmer Bill's whole dairy herd working out how to leap a four-foot fence. It had coincidentally occurred just two days after he'd publicly spurned my grandmother's completely inappropriate sexual advances, and Granny had been seething with rage and embarrassment.

It was only when the cows had finished causing havoc in the town and reached my grandmother's cottage, churning up her lawn, that the herd had decided their field was a better option after all. The police who had escorted the animals home had never worked out why the cows had suddenly turned around and headed back to their field, just as Granny hurled a tirade of abuse at them. My grandmother had tried to blame the whole incident on a low-pressure weather front coming in from the east, but my sister was adamant she'd seen Granny brewing a potion that involved milk and an energy drink.

Impressed at how far away the shouting woman could make her voice heard, I climbed the steep hundred-metre-long footpath. The gate at the top of the hill which led into the shared gardens was open, and a group of gardening enthusiasts crowded around Sam Hedgewick and his angry adversary.

I paused for a moment before stepping through the gateway. Was I being nosy? No, I decided, I was being naturally inquisitive — a quality that any good witch needed — according to my mum.

Anyway, I'd recognised the shouting woman as Hilda Cox, a normally mild mannered woman, and certainly not the sort of person who routinely made vegetable related threats of violence. Something must have really made her angry, and I *absolutely* needed to know what. How could that possibly have been construed as nosiness?

I weaved a route between the beds of vegetables and bamboo frames which bean plants covered with bright red flowers, and joined the group of spectators. I recognised a lot of them, and some of their eyes lit up when they saw I was back in town. Now was not the time to catch up with them, though — now was the time to watch a woman clutching an onion twice the size of the ones you find in supermarkets, giving a sullen faced Sam Hedegwick a dressing down.

"How could you, Sam?" yelled Hilda. "You know most of us will be lost without our allotments. We can't all afford homes with big gardens." She looked Sam up and down. "Like some people."

"Hilda," said Sam, his business suit looking as out of place amongst the vegetable patches as a cow did in a horse race. And I'd seen that. Believe me. With a grandmother like mine, I'd seen a lot. "I don't want to sell it, but I have to. You'll all get your rent back for the remainder of the year, you don't need to worry about that, but the allotments are being sold next week. That's the end of the matter."

"It's not my rent that worries me," Bill Winters, a ruddy faced man with a full head of snow white hair, chimed in. "It's the fact that I was probably going to win the largest marrow contest this year. How can you do this to me? To us? You know I've been trying to win that competition for ten years, and this year I've got it right. It's going to be a monster marrow, Sam! A monster!"

Sam looked down at his shoes and shook his head. "I'm sorry, Bill. Really, I am. There's nothing I can do. The contracts are being signed next week, and then it's up to the developers to decide how quickly they start building."

"So, my beautiful cabbages will be buried beneath posh folk's fancy apartment buildings?" said another man, much to the agreement of the grumbling crowd.

"Can you dig them up before I sell?" asked Sam, looking somewhat flustered.

"They're not ready!" spat the man. He lowered his head, and his body slumped, his voice faltering as he spoke again, "my cabbages aren't ready. They're just not ready."

A woman placed her hand on his back. "There, there, Timothy. Don't upset yourself. You know what the doctor said, no stress, and no whiskey. Oh, and no fried bacon. I must remember that one." She turned her attention to Sam. "See what you've done to him? My husband is a proud man, who grows the best cabbages in this town —"

"Easy now, Marjorie," interrupted a tall elderly

man with a stern face, leaning on a gardening fork which he twisted into the soil. "They're good cabbages, yes, but the best? I'm not so sure."

"See what you've done, Sam?" said Marjorie. "You've got us bickering amongst ourselves now!"

"I'm sorry all right!" said Sam. "I can't help you. Any of you. I'm sorry."

Several people spoke at once, and Sam's panicked face flitted between them. "What about our sheds? They cost money," said one. "And my tools. Where will I store them? I live in a tiny apartment!" pleaded another.

Sam dropped his head and turned his back to the crowd. "Sorry folks," he mumbled, and began making his way across the allotment towards the small carpark. "Really, I'm sorry."

He cut a sad figure as he meandered along the muddy paths, and I couldn't help feeling sorry for him.

"Watch your back, Sam Hedgewick!" yelled Hilda, brandishing the onion above her head like a gladiatorial weapon, her face beetroot red. "You've made a lot of people angry!"

Sam raised a hand in surrender and continued his lonely walk.

Fingers tightened on my wrist, and I turned to see the smiling face of Veronica Potter. Her make-up was as garishly applied as always, and I struggled to keep a smile off my face as I remembered my mother once referring to her as a pantomime dame. She had certainly put an awful lot of effort into getting prepared for a visit to an allotment. "It's good to see you back, Penelope!" she gushed. "I thought I heard a boat in the distance, and I said to Marjorie, 'Penelope's sister told me that she's due home this week. I wonder if it's her!'"

"It's great to be back, Veronica, but I wasn't expecting all this as I settled in for my first evening at home. I've only been back for an hour."

Veronica moved her head closer to mine. "Ignore it," she whispered. "They'll get over it. They can take up bowling or something when the allotment goes. It's only a hobby after all. It's not like they can't buy veg in the supermarket."

The other people had begun traipsing back to their plots of land since Sam had left, and I waved and said hello to the ones who greeted me.

"Why is he selling it?" I said, freeing my wrist from Veronica's surprisingly strong grasp.

"He didn't say. He just came here and broke the news." She moved her face even closer to mine. "He's a gambling man, and not a very good one, he's probably got himself in debt. Between me and you, Penelope. I don't really care. I only come here to flirt with the men. It's just a shame that most of them are at the age where they feel the cold more. It's summer, and I was hoping to at least see a few torsos."

I hid the shudder that traversed my whole body. "What about Ron? Aren't you and him still an item?"

"It's complicated, Penelope. The nursing home have a new rule in place stopping us from visiting each other's rooms after nine at night. We can get around it of course, but it's not nice to be sneaking around at my age, and then of course we're forced keep the noise down. And where's the fun in that?"

I wished I'd learnt a spell that would stop Veronica speaking, or at least one that would wash away the images that Veronica had conjured up in the darkest recesses of my mind. "It must be hard," I murmured, thinking of an excuse to get away from there. Quickly.

"Yes, well. It's not easy being old, dear. You'll see one day."

That wasn't *totally* true, but of course Veronica didn't know that. Not many people knew that real witches existed at all, and of those people, only a select handful knew about the existence of the haven. A place I was never going to get to if I believed my mother. Not that it bothered me too much at the age of twenty-three. I had plenty of time left to put in the work needed to ascend.

"Didn't Ron want to come to the allotment?" I asked. "He's usually here tending the nursing home's patch. He kept me well supplied with green beans last year."

The nursing home was not a run of the mill retirement home. It was for people who had been financially successful in life, and the allotment patch kept the kitchens supplied with the freshest of produce for the chefs to prepare outlandishly delicious meals with. The home encouraged its residents to get out into the open air and do a little gardening from time to time, and with the home being less than half a mile from the allotments, it was a relatively easy walk for the fitter of residents, and a minibus ferried the less mobile back and forth.

Last year had seen a record crop of green beans, and thanks to the kindness of the allotment owners, I'd practically lived off them — coated with a little melted butter and sprinkled with cumin seeds. It was handy having the allotment so close to my mooring, and to my shame, as well as accepting free offerings from people, I'd once or twice sneaked in under the cover of darkness and dug myself a potato to bake in the oven. To even out the universe and absolve myself from guilt, I'd cast a gentle fertility spell over the allotments which had been too late in the year to benefit last year's produce, but was certainly responsible for the size of Bill's marrows this year.

Veronica laughed. "Ron won't come here

anymore, not since they built a new gym in the home. He's always in there, pimping steel."

"Iron," I smiled, managing to swallow a giggle. "*Pumping* iron."

"Yes, that's it. You should see him though, Penelope. Big and buff, and with a line of muscles that takes the eye from his stomach, right down to his big old —"

"It's good to keep fit!" I interrupted. "Good for Ron."

"Yes, but Ron's not doing it for that reason, he's doing it to keep fresh for me, and to make sure I don't stray. I'm quite the flower amongst weeds in the home, and a lot of the men wouldn't mind walking into the breakfast room with me on their arm, and doesn't Ron know it!" Veronica giggled as my eyes widened. "He threw a pea at Wally during dinner on Tuesday because he looked at me for a little too long. He's got quite the jealous streak, but he's a real man, Penelope, and with his new muscles he struts around like a big old peacock."

Veronica gazed into the distance for a few moments with a twinkle in her eye, and I took the chance to change the subject and make my escape. "Well, it was nice seeing you, Veronica," I said. "But I have to get back to the boat. I rushed over here when I heard the shouting, and I think I...."

"Yes?"

Think Penny. Think. "...left the oven on?"

Veronica put her hand on my back and turned me in the direction of the canal. "Get back then, Penelope, hurry. I've never trusted gas. I've read too many stories about gas explosions. You don't want one of those on your boat. It would probably sink!"

I started my walk across the allotments with unwelcome images of Ron and Veronica imprinted on my mind. "See you soon, Veronica," I said, stepping over an abnormally large cauliflower. Maybe my fertility spell hadn't been gentle enough, there seemed to be some unfeasibly healthy looking vegetables growing everywhere I looked.

"Oh, Penelope!" she called. "Are you open for business?"

"I won't be opening for normal business hours, I need a break after the last four months, but if I'm home and someone stops by, they're welcome to come in."

"Oh good. All that talking about Ron has given me an idea. I need you to make me a special potion. A *very* special one."

I dodged an overturned wheelbarrow and hopped over a two-foot-long cucumber. "Pop in tomorrow if you like. I'm going into town in the morning, but I'll be home by six."

"Six o'clock it is!" said Veronica, stumbling over

dried clods of earth as she headed towards a group of men, pruning her hair as she walked.

With a final farewell, I headed back the way I'd come, and paused halfway down the footpath to appreciate my piece of paradise. The canal sparkled below me, travelling east to west, and my mooring led directly off it at a right angle. It was a tight angle to negotiate in a long boat, but under the tutelage of a friendly fellow boat owner, I'd soon learnt how to make the turn.

My sister had insisted the man had only helped me because I was blocking the canal, but I liked to think it was my first introduction to the legendary community spirit of the people who made the canals their home.

The dead-end channel of water was large enough for two boats, but home only to my canal narrowboat, and grassy slopes rose on all three sides of the cutaway, giving way to the trees which gave me seclusion.

A towpath ran along the opposite bank of the canal, and trees shrouded the side of the waterway my home was cut into, dipping their lower branches in the water.

I shouted as I descended the footpath. "Mabel! Mabel!"

She'd failed to appear when I'd arrived home, but she'd show up soon enough. She wasn't the type of goose who got on with other members of her species. She preferred human company, and certainly wouldn't put up with the two swans which were feeding in the margins of my mooring.

Rosie was leaning over the edge of the roof, hissing at them as I climbed back aboard the boat. "Come on," I said. "It's dinnertime. It's tuna Tuesday!"

She leapt down with a happy mewl, and scurried through the open bow doors. Rosie ate tuna flavoured food on most days of the week, but I tried to make it sound more special on a Thursday and a Tuesday.

I ducked as I descended the two steps into the belly of my boat. The shop section of my boat, which had been the saloon lounge when I'd bought it, was packed with various incenses and herbs — along with all the other witchcraft paraphernalia that mortal witches enjoyed trying to make magic with, and the whole boat smelled deliciously herby.

Stepping past the tiny sales counter, I breezed through the purple curtain that acted as a door, and made my way into the middle section of the sixty-foot narrowboat, the part that customers never saw. Unless they were of the nosy variety — the type of person that would scare you half to death as you looked up from reading a book, or stirring a stew, and saw them peering in through one of the large rectangle windows that ran along either side of the steel hull.

The living quarters and galley kitchen area was compact, but cosy and comfortable nonetheless. With ample seating, a fully functioning kitchen, and minimally decorated in a way that I hoped said modern *and* traditional, it was my idea of perfect. The coal and wood burner stood in the corner, unused since winter, and the space on the wall where I had intended on hanging a TV was still bare.

Beyond the living area was my bathroom, and past that, my bedroom, which was accessed by a narrow corridor. The bedroom was large enough for a compact double bed, and a pair of doors opened onto the stern decking, allowing me the pleasure of a breeze on my face as I slept on a warm summer's night. With a fire burning in the living area stove and the stern doors closed, the bedroom became a toasty warm haven on a cold winter's night.

The bathroom was small, but contained everything I needed. With white tiled walls, it boasted a full-sized shower, a sink, and a toilet. I'd decided to keep quiet about my composting toilet in the future. I'd almost been chased away from a village I'd moored up in, when I'd used it as a unique selling point to sell more of the potted herbs that dotted the flat roof of my boat. I'd never been back to the village, and I was beginning to understand how snake oil salesmen had felt.

I loved the *Water Witch*, and I loved living

between walls that were just under seven-feet apart. Who needed acres of floor space? Especially floor space that you couldn't move from scenic village to bustling town, or even busy city at the drop of a hat. No, living in a house or apartment was not for me. I liked to imagine myself as a nomadic witch, like those of the past.

With Rosie's bowls filled, and the radio switched on and placed next to an open window, I reclaimed my position on the roof. After fishing the suicidal and drunk flies from my wine glass, I took a long gulp, closed my eyes, and lay back beneath the last of the evening sun.

An hour later, and with a warm tipsiness coursing through my veins, I climbed off the roof as the sun began setting over the canal, and went inside the boat. Rosie leapt onto me as I sat down, and with her curled up on my lap, I made a few phone calls to let people know I was home, and to arrange some meet ups for the following day.

It was good to be back in Wickford, and I looked forward to not having to negotiate canal locks or worry about finding a mooring spot in a busy town on market day. With the sound of water lapping against the hull competing with Rosie's snoring, I drifted off to sleep on the sofa, to intrusive thoughts of Ron and Veronica sneaking around the nursing home in just their underwear.

CHAPTER TWO

*R*osie woke me up at precisely eight o'clock in the morning by massaging my face and mewling in my ear. "Okay," I said, gently pushing her away, and promising myself for the fiftieth time that I wouldn't fall asleep on the sofa fully clothed again. "I know. It's breakfast time."

After topping Rosie's water and food bowls up, I put some coffee on, took a shower, and dressed in a short purple dress over leggings, with my favourite oxblood Dr Martens on my feet. The short boots were years old and beginning to show their age, but shoes and clothes shopping was almost at the top of my 'things I don't enjoy in life' list — directly beneath public flatulence — but a few spots above sporks. Whoever had come up with the idea for sporks was certainly not a fan of soup or a meaty steak. Too shallow for soup, and not strong enough for a nice piece of rump, a spork was just not fit for purpose.

With a mug of black coffee in my hand, and Rosie rubbing against my legs, I tossed some stale bread to the noisy congregation of ducks and swans that had gathered around my boat. They'd soon disperse when Mabel the goose made an appearance, but for the time being they were welcome to share my mooring with me. Several of them looked up at me sullenly as I threw the last piece of dry bread to a particularly shy looking duck on the edge of the group, and set about unstrapping my bike from the front of the boat. The red bike clattered as I threw it ashore, but I'd long ago stopped worrying about scratching it, and after locking the boat up and making sure Rosie's cat flap was open, I headed off up the footpath towards town to meet my best friend.

I was due to meet Susie at nine o'clock sharp, and when Susie said sharp, she meant samurai sword sharp. Just being half a minute late would have elicited a soul wilting stare from her — even if she hadn't seen me for months. It was a quick cycle into town, and I waved at the few people who recognised me as I negotiated the almost traffic free streets of Wickford. The morning sun was already warming my face, and the older building's light coloured stonework glowed in the golden light, like the crust on a particularly good clotted cream. The scent of the freshly watered flowers that bulged from the hanging baskets beneath every wrought iron street light made me strangely happy, and I even looked forward to visiting my mother later in the day.

The imaginatively named Coffee Pot Café stood on the corner of Church Street and High Street, and after leaning my bike against the post-box outside, I went inside to a friendly welcome from Mrs Patterson, the long-term owner and baker of some of finest pastries in town.

"Penelope!" she said, "Susie said you were coming! It's great to see you."

"It's great to be back," I said, looking over the heads of the other diners for my friend.

"She's over there," said Mrs Patterson, pointing. "At the table in the corner. She's tucked away behind the Colonel and his massive newspaper. She's ordered a drink and some toast for you."

Susie was huddled at the table with a pot of tea for two, and two slices of hot buttered toast for each of us. She was well hidden by Colonel Bradshaw's newspaper, and her face lit up when she took her eyes off her phone and saw me. "Penny!" she squealed, standing up as I approached the table. "You're early! I was just about to phone you."

I gave her a wide grin and returned the bearhug she locked me in. "Pleased to see you too, Susie," I said, raising my eyebrows.

"Of course I'm pleased to see you, Penny. I just wasn't expecting you to be early."

After knowing Susie for as many years as I had, it was easy to let her obsessive time keeping go straight over my head with a smile. I sat down opposite her, wondering why I always got a seat that had one leg shorter than the others, and bit into the crispy crust of my toast while Susie poured us a cup of tea.

"So," said Susie. "How's tricks?"

It was a private joke we'd shared since we were eleven years old, when Susie had discovered my family were witches. Everyone had been using the trendy question at the time, but to me and Susie it had always had a greater meaning.

"Things are magic," I said, delivering the punchline, much to Susie's delight.

"I've missed you, Penny," she said, tucking into her toast. "Please tell me you're staying for good."

I narrowed my eyes and stared at her. "You've been talking to my mother, haven't you? She's recruited you into the '*get Penny to stop her ridiculous floating shop fantasy, and live a normal life*' team, hasn't she?"

Susie flicked a stray strand of blonde hair from her eye and tried to stifle a giggle. "Did you use magic to work that out, Penelope Weaver?" she said, keeping her voice low, as we always did when we spoke about witchy things in public.

I added another sugar to my tea. "I wish I *could* do mind reading magic, but as we all know, especially if you listen to my mother..." Susie laughed as I put on a voice, not a million miles away from my mother's high pitched whine, but closer to the sound a boy makes when he traps himself in his trouser zipper, "...I'm a witch who has absolutely no pride in her heritage, and has absolutely no chance of ascending if she continues to only focus on the element of water. A witch needs to feel the earth between her toes, just as much as she needs to be near water."

Susie did very well not to spit her tea across the table. "That's exactly what she says!"

I took another bite of toast, savouring the melted butter. Mrs Patterson sourced all her ingredients locally, and the butter was from the dairy on the outskirts of town, produced from Farmer Bill's errant cows. "Does my mother not know that a canal has banks? And occasionally I venture onto the aforementioned banks and walk around on dry land?" I said, smiling as I chewed.

"She just misses you," she said, "and Willow does. Speaking of Willow — you won't believe how tall she's got. It's like she went on a massive growth spurt the day she turned eighteen."

My heart sank. I'd wanted nothing more than to be with my sister on such a landmark birthday, but I'd been miles away, near London, moored up next to a music festival. It had been a great day for trade and I'd practically sold all my stock to the legions of women, and some men, who'd wanted to become witches. They'd have been shocked to know that the dark-haired girl who'd served them was a real witch. Not as shocked as they'd have been to find out that real witches existed, though.

"I'm gutted that I missed her birthday."

"She understands. She's really proud of you."

"I'm going straight there after breakfast to see them," I said. "I wanted to pick some flowers up for mum first."

Susie sipped her tea. "I hope she likes cheap flowers from the convenience store."

"Why?"

"There's a passive aggressive handwritten sign in the florist's window," said Susie, picking up her phone and showing me the screen. "Look, I took a photo. In my line of work, it pays to keep your finger on the pulse."

I took the phone from Susie and read the sign.

'It is with deep regret that I must inform my customers that this shop is closing down. You can thank the town's most successful businessman and all-round nice person — Mr Sam Hedgewick, for the inconvenience to yourselves, and the life altering change in my circumstances.

He has been kind enough to give me a full three days' notice that he is selling the property, and I must vacate it immediately. Thanks to an exceptionally well written contract, which Mr Hedgewick was kind enough to read aloud to me, I have no legal leg to stand on.

Please show Mr Hedgewick your appreciation when you next pass him in the street, or when he crosses the road in front of your car.'

I passed the phone back to Susie with a frown. "Sam's ruffling a few feathers."

Susie narrowed her eyes. "A few?"

I told her about the incident in the allotments, leaving out my conversation with Veronica. There were better places than at the breakfast table for talking about randy elderly folk.

"I wonder what he's playing at," Susie said. "I'm going to look into it."

I swallowed the toast in my mouth and took another bite. "Investigative journalism. At least some reporters still practice it."

Susie smiled. "I have to, I'm a freelance journalist. Not many newspapers will pay for a story about a vandalised bus stop in Wickford. Between this Sam Hedgewick thing and the car show, I'll probably be able to sell a story to The Herald."

"Car show?" I said.

Susie poured the last of the tea, sharing it between us. It was hardly worth adding sugar to the inch of liquid in my cup.

"You've come back just in time, Penny. It's a vintage car show, you'll see loads of old cars on the roads in the next few days, and the local businesses will make more money this week than they have in months. Some of the cars are real beauties, even to someone like me who can't tell a Rolls Royce and a Mini apart. They've hired the big camping field next to the canal on the outskirts of town. There's a big marquee too with a bar and live music. I think the whole things just an excuse to get drunk to be honest. You should moor your boat there. You'll make a lot of money."

I shook my head. "No. I'm staying right where I'm moored for now. I need a break."

"Fair enough," said Susie. "It will probably be more of a man thing anyway, maybe not your target customers."

"You'd be surprised," I said. "There's more men into witchcraft than people imagine."

"Probably trying to conjure up a few more inches down there," Susie laughed, her hair falling into her eyes. She waved it away and drank the last of her tea. "Or trying to magic themselves into some tarts underwear while their fiancée is at home planning their wedding."

I raised my eyebrows and gave a theatrical sigh. "I'd have thought an independent woman like you would have been over a waste of skin like him a long time ago."

Susie giggled. "Oh, I'm over Robert. Don't you worry about that. It doesn't hurt to laugh about him now and again though. I mean, what sort of man pays for tablets from China that promise to grow his pride and joy an inch or two overnight? And to think he was taking them to try and impress that tart!"

I laughed hard from my belly, and the table shook, nearly knocking the teapot over the edge. "I shouldn't laugh. It sounds like he was very poorly. God knows what was in those pills."

"Bath salts I imagine. Or some type of acid. He thought he had two heads at one point and tried to drown the imposter in the bath. It's a good job I found him, he was almost out of breath."

Our loud giggles drew the attention of some of the other diners, and we calmed ourselves down with deep breaths. I'd been on my canal travels when the Robert incident had occurred, and Susie managed to remember something new every time we spoke about it. The bath story was new to me, and possibly one of the funniest she'd told me yet. Not for Robert though. He'd spent a night in a mental health facility, and hadn't fully recovered for weeks.

When we'd calmed ourselves down, Susie asked

about my trip, listening intently as I told her about all the people I'd met and the places I'd been. "I almost sold out completely last week," I answered, when she asked me about business. "I stopped off and restocked on my way home, so my shelves are full again."

"I'm so happy for you, I knew you could do it," said Susie reaching for the bag at her feet. "I'm really sorry I can't stay longer, but I need to go and do some work. Do you want me to take you to the florists in Covenhill first? My cars parked around the corner."

"No thanks," I said. "I'll buy some pastries from Mrs Patterson. Mum loves the cinnamon and raisin ones. She'll enjoy them more than flowers. She thinks flowers are for funerals and cheating husbands."

"You mentioned something about free steak when you phoned last night," hinted Susie with a grin. "Is the invitation still open?"

"Definitely! I'll pick up some meat from the butchers on my way back to the boat. I'm going to invite Willow and Mum too. Willow loves barbecues, but Mum will say no – she has a thing about accidentally eating insects. She has to inspect her bedroom every night for spiders. She thinks they lower themselves into people's mouths while they sleep."

Susie spoke in hushed tones. "And to think that woman is a powerful witch," she said. "I'd have thought she'd embrace spiders." She leaned down and gave me a hug. "It's great to have you back, Penny. I'll see you tonight, and I'll bring some wine."

"No need. I've got plenty of my homemade stuff left."

Susie smirked. "That's why I'm bringing my own."

CHAPTER THREE

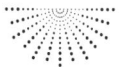

With a bag of pastries in the small basket on the front of my bike, I took the narrow lane that led north-east out of the small market town. The mile-long trip to my childhood home was all uphill, and the tall hedgerows were alive with singing birds, with wild strawberry plants dotting the grass verges. Resisting the temptation to stop and pick some, I took the right turn onto the long gravel path that led through my mother's private woodland, and smiled as Hazelwood cottage appeared around the bend. The garden, and the climbing roses that crawled up the cottage's white walls, were in full bloom, and I sniffed the scented air happily as I wheeled my bike up the pathway.

The thick oak door swung open as I approached it, and my sister ran out to greet me, dressed in shorts, a tight white t-shirt, and a pair of flip-flops. "Penny!" she shouted, hugging me so tightly I nearly dropped my bike.

I returned her hug one with one arm, and looked her up and down as she took a step backwards. I gave a low whistle. "Wow," I said. "You've blossomed."

"So I'm told," she laughed. "Quick, come inside, Mum's going to be back soon."

Mum's little car was still parked beneath the large beech tree alongside the cottage, so I guessed she hadn't taken a trip into town. "She's in the haven?"

"Yeah, come inside quickly, we can watch her coming back."

Willow led me into the cottage, and a flash of silver on her wrist caught my attention as she closed the door behind us. "You got my present then?" I said. "I'm sorry I wasn't here for your birthday."

"You can make up for it next year," she smiled, "but I love my bracelet! Thank you!" The silver bracelet, complete with the cat and wand charms I'd added, jangled as she held it out for me to inspect. "Look, I bought another charm."

"A cauldron, it's lovely."

Willow narrowed her eyes. "Seriously though, Penny... did you put any *real* charms on it? Of the magical variety? I can't detect any, but I'm pretty sure you have."

I shook my head. "No, I promise. I wouldn't cast a

spell on of anything of yours without telling you. Why do you ask?"

I followed Willow down the hallway towards the kitchen, fascinated by how her backside had filled out in the time since I'd last seen her. When I'd left four months ago, she'd been stick thin — nothing like the curvy young woman she'd become.

Willow sat at the large wooden table and pulled a seat out for me. "It's just that since I've been wearing it, I've had a lot of male attention, much more than normal. Something's not right. I thought you'd put an attraction spell on it."

I placed the bag of pastries on the table and pointed at my sister's chest. "I think it's got more to do with those than any magic tricks," I smirked. "Those are the only attraction spells you need. How did they get so big so quickly?"

My sister gazed down at herself, her cheeks blushing red. "Mum calls them my devil's dumplings."

My laughter echoed around the kitchen, and Willow joined in, her body shaking.

"Mum's just jealous," I said when I'd managed to stop laughing. "Granny told me she used to stuff her bras when she was younger."

Willow opened her mouth to say something, but put her finger over her lips instead. "Stop talking about Mum, she's back," she said, nodding towards the lounge.

I turned to face the open doorway. Although I'd seen Mum entering and leaving the haven hundreds of times, the trick never grew old. The crooked doorway quivered and creaked, and the edges began glowing white as a hovering light appeared in the centre. It spread outward until the space was filled with bright blue light, that made a low humming sound as it rippled like the surface of a pond on a windy day.

A large chocolate covered cake on a tray appeared through the light, held by hands on the end of arms that were cut off at the elbows by the shimmering sheet of blue. "Take care, Eva!" came Mum's voice, throbbing in time with the humming of the spell. "Don't do anything I wouldn't do!"

"You know me, Maggie, always on my best behaviour!" came the distant reply.

With her long hair standing on end, the tips sparking with flashes of red, the rest of my mother emerged through the doorway as the light faded and disappeared behind her. The humming stopped immediately, and my mother gazed at us in turn. "Penelope, you're home. I hope you're hungry. Aunt Eva made a cake."

"I brought pastries," I said, tapping the paper bag in front of me

Mum smiled. "How nice," she said, placing the

huge cake on the table next to my meagre offering. "Perhaps I'll try one later."

Willow giggled. "Mum, your hair's smoking."

Mum nodded. "Thank you, dear."

"No, I didn't mean it like that. It's actually smoking," said Willow, pointing at the smouldering strands of hair that framed Mum's plump face.

Mum frantically patted her head. "I'll have split ends!" she said. "It's because I brought the cake through. Eva put a little magic in it to make it taste better, bringing magic through the portal messes with the space-time continuum."

"Mum's been watching Star Trek re-runs," whispered Willow, as my mother extinguished the last of the embers that fell onto her shoulders. "It's not a space-time continuum, Mum. It's because there's too much of Eva's magic in the cake for this world. The portal just evened it out a little."

The type of magic that could be used in the haven was far older than magic in the real world, and any magic that came through from the other dimension was severely weakened by the portal. The safeguards were put in place after the portal wars of 1907, which left twelve people in our world transformed into toads. They now languished in a purpose-built pond in the haven, surrounded by only the most succulent of flies.

"I know that, young lady!" snapped Mum. "I'm

just trying to make magic sound more exciting to you two girls. Today's young generation of witches don't care about magic like we used to when I was younger. You're more interested in boys and make-up."

My eyes widened and Willow's jaw dropped. "That's hardly fair," I protested. "I haven't had a proper boyfriend since I was nineteen, and when do you see me wearing more than a little lip gloss?"

Mum opened one of the large cupboards that lined the kitchen walls. She retrieved four plates and took a large knife from a drawer. "Well maybe not so much you, Penelope," she said, placing a plate each in front of me and Willow and laying the knife next to the cake. "You're too busy floating around the countryside in that death trap of yours, selling fake magic to desperate people who can't find love the old-fashioned way. Your sister on the other hand..." She didn't finish her sentence, she just pursed her lips, raised her eyebrows, and shook her head gently.

"Yes?" said Willow, "go on, what about me?"

Mum turned to me. "Since your sister grew those fun pillows, she's been parading herself around town, pushing her chest out, and acting puzzled when men suddenly start wanting to give her their phone numbers."

"I do not!" said Willow, placing her arms protectively across her chest.

The two of them stared at me as I burst into laughter.

"What's so funny?" said Mum.

"It's just good to be back," I said truthfully. "Come on, let's have some cake."

Mum sat down and pointed at the fourth plate. "We won't cut it until your grandmother gets here."

"Fun pillows," muttered Willow under her breath.

"Granny's coming?" I asked. "How is she?"

"Your sister hasn't told you?"

Willow moved a finger towards the bulging layer of sticky chocolate that covered the cake. "You told me not to tell her," she said.

"When do you ever do anything I ask you to?" said Mum, knocking Willow's hand away. "It's not good news I'm afraid, Penelope."

My heart sank.

"She's got witch dementia."

My heart lifted again. "That's not too bad," I said. "She'll soon get over it."

Mum fixed me with a stern stare, the frazzled hair hanging around her face making her look far less imposing than she was trying to be. "That's not very nice, Penelope. Imagine having your spells mixed up. Last week she tried to make one of her chickens lay bigger eggs, but she accidentally used a spell meant for an ostrich. That poor chicken... and the ones who witnessed it."

"It got better," said Willow, gazing at the cake. "It still looks a little shocked though."

"It's dangerous for other people, and scary for your Grandmother," said Mum. "The sooner it wears off, the better."

"How long has she had it?" I said.

"Since the accident with that goose of yours."

I sat up straighter in my seat. "What accident? Granny told me she did that because Mabel stole her sandwich. She said she'd reverse the spell as soon as she'd learned her lesson."

Mum dropped her eyes and fiddled with the top button of her long flowery dress. "She was ashamed. She'd tried to cast a spell to clamp its beak closed for an hour or so, but.... well, you know what happened."

Didn't I just — and so did the other waterfowl that used to share my little piece of water with her. Any sensible duck wouldn't come within a hundred metres of my mooring spot these days when Mabel was around. I'd thought Granny's spell had been a little extreme for the simple crime of sandwich theft by waterfowl. It made sense now. Granny had gone very quiet after cursing Mabel, and hadn't stayed around for the fruit trifle, which was very unlike my food loving grandmother.

"Anyway," Mum continued. "She's very angry about the whole thing. She just wants to get back to normal."

Willow agreed. "She can't even get to the haven to be cured. She's forgotten her entry spell. She blew a door off a changing room cubicle in a clothes shop when she tried."

I frowned. "Why on earth would she use a changing cubicle door to enter the haven? It's a very public place to be doing magic."

Mum stood up and crossed the kitchen. She brushed some hanging bunches of dried herbs away from one of the cupboard doors, and got the teapot out. She added some teabags to the huge pot and filled it with water from the kettle that whistled on the old aga stove. "She was trying on a new dress and she wanted Aunt Eva's opinion. The changing rooms were empty. Until the explosion anyway."

Willow laughed, and I couldn't help joining in.

"It's not funny, you two," Mum scolded, her wide hips swaying as she carried the teapot to the table. "At least your grandmother got her entry spell when she was nice and young, the way you two are going, you'll be lucky to get yours before you die! You need to take your magic more seriously. You're getting too wrapped up with what's going on in this world."

Since each of us had turned ten years old, our mother had been insisting we'd never work hard enough to ascend. Mum had acquired her ascension spell at the age of twenty-one, and whenever she entered the haven, that was the age she'd be while there. She could live to be a hundred in the mortal world, but as long as she entered the haven permanently before she died, she would always be twenty-one in the magical dimension.

Aunt Eva had been aged eighty-nine when she'd decided to permanently move to the haven, and she now enjoyed immortality in the body of a nineteen-year-old. She could never come back to our world, but we could go and visit her. If we ever ascended that is.

Each person's entry spell was different, and when a witch had gained enough magical knowledge to ascend, the spell would be made known to them. When a witch had acquired their spell, they could use any door or entrance to conjure a portal.

Mum's chair creaked as she sat down. "I've got more hope for Willow than I have for you, Penelope. At least she practices, and she's getting to know all the elements. You're stuck in that floating tin, surrounded by water for most of the time. You're like a goldfish."

Try as I might, I couldn't work out how living in a boat could be equated with being like a fish. Perhaps if I lived beneath the water in a submarine... maybe. "Why am I like a goldfish?" I asked her as she poured me a cup of tea.

She tilted her head and adopted a smug expression as she explained her theory. "What happens to a goldfish when it lives in a small bowl? It never grows, that's what happens. If you took it out of the bowl and put it a pond, it would grow to its full potential. You're the goldfish and your boat is the bowl. You'll never grow. You're not getting to know all the elements, Penelope. You need to step into a bigger pond."

I sighed. This again. "I have plenty of air. I have a fire in my boat. I live on water, and I feel the earth under my feet every time I moor up. I do just fine with the elements, thank you very much."

Mum wouldn't give up, and I sipped my tea and rolled my eyes as I listened to her. "You can't concentrate on one element more than the others, Penelope. I'm just concerned that you'll never understand the spirit element if you stay on that boat. You need to embrace the four earthly elements before you understand the spirit element, and it's the spirit element that will get you into the haven."

The sound of a car outside caught Mum's attention, halting her lecture — although I was fully aware she'd probably never give up on getting me back on dry land. Willow stood up to look through the window. "Granny's here!" she said.

The front door opened and Granny's hurried footsteps clattered down the hallway. She may have had witch dementia, but she was still three times as nimble as most women approaching eighty. She breezed into the kitchen, smiling at me before staring at my mother intently. She peered over her plastic rimmed purple glasses, inspecting Mum's charred hair, and sat down. "You've burnt your hair, Maggie. You'll need to trim and dye it."

"I don't dye my hair!" Mum said incredulously. She waved a hand between me and Willow. "I'm as naturally dark as these two!"

"Enough of your problems, dear," said Granny, her blue rinse perm looking as perfect as ever. "Penelope's home. Come and give your grandmother a kiss, I've missed you."

Granny puckered her lips as I approached her, and the smell of moth balls grew stronger as I bent down and gave her a hug, the hairs above her top lip tickling me as she planted a firm kiss on my cheek.

"And you, Willow," said Granny. "There's plenty of my loving to go around."

I heaved a sigh of relief as Willow hugged her — Mum might stop trying to talk me out of canal boat living now Granny was around. Granny had been ecstatic when I'd bought a boat, and she'd come on my first day trip with Willow, asking dozens of questions about the *Water Witch*, and offering loads of suggestions as to how I could improve her. I'd taken her advice on a lot of points, especially her idea of installing wine making equipment.

Willow sat down and Mum began cutting the

cake. It bulged at the edges as the knife sliced through the thick layer of chocolate.

"A little smaller," said Granny, watching Mum cut the first slice.

"This is my piece," said Mum.

Granny smiled. "I know, dear."

Mum was about to protest, but Granny spoke over her. "So, Penelope. How's life on the boat? I hope you're remembering to grease your stern gland regularly?"

"Enough of that!" said Mum, sliding a cake laden plate in front of Granny. "You know we don't speak about women's problems at the table. It's uncouth."

"It's part of the boat!" I laughed. "It keeps the propeller shaft watertight. I kept forgetting to grease it last year."

Granny looked happy with herself. "You'd have known that if you took the time to go on a trip with her, Maggie."

Mum ignored her and bit into her cake as she watched me take a bite of mine. My head throbbed as the cake hit my stomach, and I knew right away that the magic Aunt Eva had added to the mix was not to enhance the taste. It was a spell. Aimed at me. Images of sunny meadows and frolicking lambs swirled through my mind, with happy people in the background walking in and out of cottages in a picture-perfect village. The pleasant images faded into blackness and were immediately replaced with images of ships and boats sinking, with vicious sharks swirling through the waves below them.

The portal had obviously removed most of the spell, because almost as soon as the images had appeared, they were gone, and I still wanted to live aboard my boat.

"How do you feel?" said Mum, a crumb of cake attached to her bottom lip. "Is the cake nice?"

"You mean did the spell work?" I said. "No, it didn't, although it was quite imaginative. You can tell Aunt Eva that sharks don't live in canals, though. Sorry, but I still want to live on my boat."

"You tried to hex your own daughter!" said Granny, although she was a fine one to talk. She'd once put a spell on my mother that had guided her to the weight loss aisles of the supermarket every time she went shopping.

"I didn't. It was Eva," Mum mumbled.

"Just because you won't do the dirty work yourself, doesn't mean you're not as involved as that sister of mine," scolded Granny. "Getting somebody else to do it doesn't make you any less guilty. Anyway, you should know magic won't fully survive the trip home from the haven. If it could you would have brought something back to cure me by now."

"Oh yes, Granny," I said, changing the subject. It was best to ignore Mum. My mother trying to get me off the boat was nothing new, and the use of a spell was not unprecedented. She'd once given me a chilli flavoured toffee that she'd brought back from the haven, and it had taken me a few hours to get over my newly acquired fear of the dragonflies that lived on the canal. "How are you?" I continued. "Mum told me about your... problem."

"I'm fine," she said, "I'm sure it will wear off soon. I don't really like talking about it to be honest, it's a nuisance. I had another little accident this morning."

"Are you okay?" Willow asked with concern on her face.

"Oh, I'm perfectly fine, dear. Boris is a little shaken up though. He's a tough old goat, but even he's got his limits."

Mum raised her eyebrows. "What have you done to Boris?"

"Not me, Maggie. It was the dementia. You shouldn't label a person as their disability. It's ableism."

"Okay," said Mum, looking perplexed. "What's the *dementia* done to Boris?"

"That's better, Maggie. It's never nice to be intolerant." Granny took a sip of tea and adjusted her glasses. "I was mowing my lawn, the part that Boris won't eat due to the terrible smells those naughty cows left on it." She ignored our chorus of sighs and carried on talking. "I put a spell on the lawnmower, but the dementia got it muddled up. Instead of cutting the grass, it chased Boris in circles around his pole until the rope ran out."

"Is he okay?" I asked.

"He's fine, a little shaken up, but the big pile of hay I left for him is cheering him up." She stirred her tea. "The hair will grow back soon enough."

Willow and I exchanged glances, and my sister hid a smile. Poor Boris. It was true what Granny had said though – he was a tough old goat. He'd soon bounce back.

Granny continued. "Then I nearly got knocked down by an old-fashioned car in town when I went to the post office, there's loads of them, all heading out into the country for some sort of show."

"Yeah," I said, "Susie mentioned it."

"Well, they should be more considerate, driving around town like toad of toad hall with their hats and goggles on, they'll kill someone," said Granny.

I pushed my empty plate away from me, smiling as my mother offered me another slice. "The spell won't work any better if I eat another piece," I said, "anyway, I'm full."

"Then I witnessed an argument," continued Granny. "Sam Hedgewick was coming out of the lawyer's office and he was accosted by a badboy, he was using all sorts of naughty words. Even the bad one, and I don't mean f — "

"A *badboy*?" I interrupted. Granny must have been at Willow's contemporary romance books again.

"Yes, you know the type — tattoos, short hair, and lots of muscles. The type I'd have ended up with if I hadn't married Norman. Rest his soul." Granny's eyes widened. "Maggie!" she said. "Did you check there were no nuts in this cake?"

"Yes, and for the last time, none of us are allergic to them, and Dad choked on a whole brazil nut. He wasn't allergic to them."

"Well, if dying from something doesn't make you allergic to it, I don't know what does," said Granny. "Anyway, Penelope, that young policeman who who's got a thing for you broke the argument up and sent them both on their way."

"Barney? He hasn't got a thing for me." Granny and Willow laughed, and my cheeks warmed. "He hasn't," I protested. "Maybe in school, yes, but not anymore!"

"I agree with Penelope, I don't think he's into her," said Mum, much to my surprise. "I know he doesn't speak like one, but with that fabulous hair, and the way he walks, I think he's..." she lowered her voice. "...One. Of. Them."

Tea flew from my mouth. "Mum!" I said. "You can't say that!"

"You're being very intolerant today, Maggie," mumbled Granny through a mouthful of cake. "I'm quite ashamed. I didn't bring you up to be like that."

"Especially considering that your brother is *one of them*," I said.

Mum looked wounded. "Brian's not Scottish!"

"I thought you meant Barney was gay," I said, confused by all of what my mother had just said.

"What do you mean, Mum?" said Willow, looking as bemused as I felt. "Fabulous hair, and the way he walks?"

"That bright red hair of his — it's fabulous, and very Scottish. And the way he walks with that cocky swagger, that's very, *very* Scottish."

"He's not swaggering," I said. "It's because of his height. It's hard for him to get trousers that fit properly, they dig into his... you know."

"Love plums," said Granny, cutting herself more cake. "He needs to take care of them if you and he are going to be an item."

"We're not!" I said. "I don't understand, Mum. What have you got against the Scottish?"

"I've got nothing against the mortal Scottish, but there's a reason Shakespeare wrote Macbeth. Those evil witch hags up there in the north give us all a bad name."

Willow giggled. "But why wouldn't a Scottish person be into Penelope?"

Mum stood up and began clearing the plates away. "Because they're fighters, not lovers. Have you neither of you watched *Braveheart* or *Trainspotting*?"

"What *are* you talking about?" I said.

Mum turned her back to us and took the empty plates to the sink. "I don't want to speak about it anymore. Haven't you two girls got something better to do than gang up on me with your grandmother?"

"No one's ganging up on anyone," I said, "but no, I've got nothing to do until later. I've got to make a potion for Veronica Potter, and then I'm having a barbecue which you're all invited too, naturally."

"What potion does that painted harlot want?" said Mum.

I bit my lip. "Veronica's lovely," I said. "She wants a potion for Ron, I'm not sure what yet."

"Don't you go putting real magic in it, Penelope," said Granny.

"Of course not, I'd never do that," I said. "I just give my customers what any mortal witch can give — hope, and a bit of a show."

"I'll never understand why a real witch pretends to be a fake witch," said Mum.

"She's hiding in plain sight," said Willow. "I think it's perfect, and yes, Penny, I'd love to come to a barbecue."

"Mum, Granny?" I asked.

"Not me," said Mum. "There are too many mayflies near the canal."

"They already hatched," I said, "and they only live for a few hours. They won't hatch again for a few months."

"My point precisely," said Mum, washing the plates, her arms deep in soapy suds. "If any *did* survive, they'd be monsters by now. I can't risk one of them landing on my burger, I might not see it, and you know how I feel about eating insects."

"Granny? Do you fancy a nice piece of steak?" I said, not bothering to argue with my mother. She'd once declined an invitation to a cousin's wedding because butterflies were being released as the couple said their vows.

"I can't, sweetheart. I've got a gentleman caller coming."

Mum turned to face us, dripping water over the slate floor. "Oh?"

"Tell us more," teased Willow, leaning across the table towards Granny.

"It's not like that. I'll never love again after Norman. Rest his soul. I've got a Chinese gentleman coming to stick needles in me. I'm hoping he can unblock my spells. They say Chinese medicine is the closest thing on earth to real magic."

"You'd better keep that magic of yours under control," said Mum. "No spells at all while he's at your cottage, do you hear me? Who knows what could happen."

"I hear you loud and clear," smirked Granny, doing absolutely nothing to convince me.

"Anyway," said Mum. "What do you mean — you'll never love again after Dad? Have you forgotten about Bill?"

"I do not like that terrible man!" said Granny, her glasses sliding the full length of her nose. "I've said it a hundred times, but I'll say it once more in the hope it will stick in those empty heads of yours." She leaned over the table and looked at each of us in turn as she spoke. "Farmer Bill dropped a mouthful of food into his lap and I was just trying to pick it up for him. His reaction in front of everybody in the cafe was over the top, and I certainly did nothing to his cows. That's the last I'll say on the matter!"

The three of us rolled our eyes at each other. "Okay, Granny," I said. "We believe you."

"Speak for yourself," mumbled Willow. "I know what I saw."

"Right! That's enough of that backchat, Willow!" Granny's face clouded over and she scrunched her features into a porcine scowl.

"No Granny! You've got dementia!" I shouted.

It was too late. Granny clicked her fingers and the audible sizzle that accompanied spells cast in anger vibrated through the air.

Willow shuddered and looked down at her body. "No!" she shouted. "Why would you do that Granny?"

Granny's face transformed from angry to worried in less than a second. "I'm so sorry, my darling," she panicked. "I just wanted to shrink those wonderful boobies of yours for an hour or two. I must have got my spells muddled up."

Mum stood behind Willow and put her hand on her head, testing the strength of the spell. "Don't worry, dear," she soothed. "It's not too powerful. It'll only last for a day, and I'm sure you'll be able to hide them."

CHAPTER FOUR

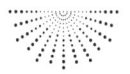

It had been an eventful day at Mum's house, but finally It was time to leave. Veronica was due at my boat in an hour, and I needed to stop off in town to pick up supplies for the barbecue.

"I'd better drive," I said, putting my bike in the back of Mum's car.

Willow nodded, looking down at her feet. "I can't believe she did it."

"You girls look after my car!" shouted Mum from the cottage doorway. "And don't let Willow drive, Penelope. She can hardly walk properly, let alone use the brake pedal."

Willow made a strangled sound which was almost a sob. "I'm not going to drive, Mum," she shouted.

"That's the least of my worries — it's summer and I can't even wear my flip-flops, thanks to Granny!"

Mum gave us a wave and began closing the cottage door. She shouted some final encouragement. "Maybe it's a good thing, darling. It will stop you obsessing about those flesh jellies of yours for a day or two."

The door had already closed, so Mum didn't hear Willow's shouted reply. The birds did though, and several flew from the tall trees surrounding the cottage, squawking in offence at Willow's choice of language.

"You'll get the hang of walking," I said as we got in the car. "Are they comfortable?"

Wracked with guilt, Granny had carved two thin pieces of wood into the shape and size Willow's feet had once been, and taped them to her new baby sized feet. With kitchen sponges glued to the toe end of the wood, Willow could wear a pair of trainers, although balancing was a problem.

"I suppose," grunted Willow. "Come on let's get to your boat. I need wine."

The trip into town only took a few minutes, but negotiating the streets of Wickford took longer. With vintage cars everywhere, and the pavements packed with people admiring the old vehicles, it took over half an hour to find a parking space and get the supplies I needed from the parade of shops on High Street.

Susie had been right — the old cars *were* beautiful, and with the drivers dressed in clothing from the same era as their machines, it was like stepping back in time.

With ten minutes left before Veronica was due at my boat, I parked in the Poacher's Pocket Hotel car park, and helped Willow out of the car before grabbing the bags of shopping from the back seat, leaving the bike where it was. Willow and Susie were staying on my boat for the night, and I'd need my bike to get back from Mum's when I took my sister home the next day.

Michelle, one half of the married couple that owned the hotel, appeared in the rear doorway of the old building, waving at us as we made our way through the beer garden to the footpath that led down to my boat. "Hi girls!" she shouted. "It's good to see you back, Penelope! Me and Tony came down to say hello earlier but you weren't there."

"Hi Michelle!" I answered. "It's good to be back. I've been at Mums all day."

"We'll come down and see you when it's not so busy," she said, waving her arm to indicate the crowds of people that sat in the garden drinking beer and wine.

"Okay, and thank whoever it was that mowed the grass for me. It was nice to come back to a neat and tidy mooring."

"Oh, that wasn't us, sweetheart. We've been far too busy with the hotel. It was Barney. He did it yesterday, he said your Granny told him you were due home any day."

Willow tittered under her breath. "Told you he likes you."

"You just concentrate on balancing," I said. "You look like you're drunk."

Willow planted her feet a little further apart, but still swayed from side to side as I said goodbye to Michelle. I held both bags in one hand and tucked my other arm through Willow's, helping her through the beer garden and down the shaded woodland footpath towards the boat.

"What was that noise?" said Willow as we neared the bottom of the path.

"Oh no!" I said. "It's Mabel, and it sounds like Veronica's here too. She's early."

I left Willow to negotiate the last of the footpath alone, and hurried ahead, the sound of barking getting louder as I neared the mooring.

"Get away from me, you monster!" came Veronica's shrill cry.

The trees gave way to freshly mown grass, and I clamped my hand over my mouth as one of the funniest sights I'd ever seen unfolded before my eyes. Veronica was standing on top of one of the picnic benches, swinging her bag at the goose who was attempting to leap up at her. Mabel had never been able to fly due to a condition the vet had called angel wing, but it didn't stop her trying. She jumped up at Veronica again, but Veronica's swinging bag prevented her from getting onto the bench top.

"Get away you beast!" shouted Veronica, much to the annoyance of Mabel, who barked and growled even louder.

Willow giggled as she entered the clearing and stood by my side. "You'd better help her," she said. "We don't want her getting hurt."

I dropped the bags at Willow's feet, and ran across the clearing. "No, Mabel," I shouted. "Leave her alone!"

Mabel looked at me and gave an excited yap, before turning her attention back to her captive victim.

"Help me, Penelope," begged Veronica, teetering on the edge of the table. "I'm too young to die."

Swallowing my laughter, I put myself between Veronica and the goose. "Sit, Mabel!" I shouted. "Sit!"

Mabel whined and tried to look past me at Veronica, who crouched behind my back with her hands on my shoulders. "Sit!" I repeated. "Do you want a treat?"

The white goose immediately sat down on her tail, with her bright orange feet sticking out in front of her.

"Good girl, Mabel," said Willow, arriving at the bench, a bag in each hand acting as counter weights which helped her balance.

"Give her a piece of ham," I said.

Willow retrieved the packet of ham from one of the bags and ripped it open. "Here, Veronica," she said, handing a slice to the shaking woman. "You give it to her, she'll be your friend forever."

"Oh my," said Veronica, leaning over the side of the table, swinging the ham in front of Mabel. "Here you are, you vicious little creature."

Mabel stood up and snatched the ham from Veronicas fingers, swallowing it whole. She gave a contented yap and lay on her back. "You can get down," I said, bending over to tickle the goose's belly. "She's your friend now."

Veronica climbed off the table with Willow's help, adjusting her bright red skirt as she stepped onto the grass. "I've never been so scared," she said. "Are you sure the vet was right, Penelope? It seems more than a voice box problem to me. She thinks she's a dog."

When a family out for a picnic had stumbled on Mabel worrying sheep in a field, they'd caught her and taken her to the vet, with the videos they'd recorded going viral on the internet. The vet, after much head scratching and research, had proclaimed that Mabel had an elongated voice box, and was probably a little simple. The newspapers had lost interest after a week or so, and Mabel had lived in relative peace ever since.

"Yes, the vet was right. It's quite common, apparently," I lied. "In some countries."

"But, look," said Veronica. "She's doing a poo with her leg cocked."

"Not there, Mabel," scolded Willow. "Not next to Penny's boat."

Mabel finished what she was doing, sniffed her deposit, and ran in a circle chasing her tail. Veronica jumped in fright as the goose barked and sprinted across the clearing towards the canal, where two unlucky swans had glided into view. "It doesn't seem right to me, Penelope," Veronica said. "Perhaps you should have another vet look at her. Geese don't eat ham for a start."

"Geese eat anything," I said. "They're greedy. Come on, let's get you into the boat, make you a nice cup of tea, and brew up this mystery potion for Ron. Mabel won't be back for a few hours, she'll chase those swans all the way to Covenhill, or until they fly away."

"Oh, you've painted your boat," said Veronica, cheering up as I led her aboard. "I didn't notice when I got here, I was too preoccupied with that... goose."

"And you've had the name repainted," observed Willow.

"I had it done last month," I said proudly. "It's all hand painted."

The boat's paintwork had been fading when I'd gone off on my four-month trip, but now it was a bright and cheerful red, with a green stripe along the centre. The hand painted name shone gold in the sun, and I smiled as I remembered the man who'd done it ask me jokingly if I'd curse him if he spelt it incorrectly. How little he knew.

Water Witch was written in large letters in a scrolling font, and beneath it in a plainer font — *Floating emporium of magick.*

"It looks lovely, dear," said Veronica, as I opened the door and led her down into the shop section.

"Willow, would you get Veronica a seat, please. I'll make her a cup of tea and check on Rosie, she's probably cowering in a corner somewhere. She's terrified of Mabel," I said.

Leaving Willow to make Veronica comfortable, I found Rosie hiding behind a wicker chair and cheered her up with a bowl of food. "You should stick up for yourself, Rosie," I said. "Granny may have made Mabel act like a dog, but she can't hurt you. She's all bark and no bite. Literally."

Rosie ignored me and got on with the important job of emptying her food bowl as I made Veronica some tea. A knock on the window behind me made me jump, and I turned around to see Susie staring down at me, a big smile on her face, and her blond hair swept back in a ponytail. She held up two bottles of wine and grinned. Never mind. I liked my elderberry wine, and if she wasn't drinking it there was more for me, and Willow — now she was old enough to drink.

"Come in," I shouted, "Veronica and Willow are in the shop."

With a cup of tea for Veronica, I made my way along the boat. Willow had set up my consulting table in the narrow space between the shelves on both hull walls, and Veronica was seated on one side of the small round table, with an empty seat ready for me on the other side. My smallest cast iron cauldron was in the middle of the table, on top of the small gas camping stove that I'd painted black with silver stars. People expected a show when they came to my shop for a potion, and painting the stove was the first thing I'd done.

Willow and Susie were behind Veronica, sitting tightly squeezed together on the steps that led onto the bow deck, and both had smiles on their faces. They enjoyed watching me make fake magic, and I was sure they were just as inquisitive as I was about what sort of potion Veronica wanted for Ron.

"Here's your tea," I said, handing Veronica the cup and saucer. "It's nice and sweet. Now... what can I help you with?"

Veronica looked over her shoulder at Willow and Susie, and then back at me. "Nothing I say will leave this boat?"

"You have my word," I said, as Willow and Susie made their promises too.

Veronica took a sip of tea and placed the cup back on the saucer. "Well, it's Ron," she said. "You know I told you he was doing all that exercise?"

I nodded.

"It's taking it out of him, Penelope... in other ways."

"Go on," I said.

Veronica bit her bottom lip, leaving a smudge of bright red lipstick on her teeth. "How do I put this?" she said. "He's having problems with... he's struggling to..."

"Yes?" I urged.

She sighed. "Snoopy won't sit up and beg."

I swallowed hard and took a deep breath. "Snoopy won't what?"

She clasped her hands together and looked me in the eyes. "Ron's little guardsman won't stand to attention, Penelope."

Willow and Susie shook with suppressed laughter, and I struggled to breathe. "So, you need a passion potion?"

"Will that put lead in his pencil?"

"I can't promise anything, Veronica," I said. "All I can do is try. Passion is a very tricky thing. Maybe I can add something that will help him get more rest too, maybe he's tired out after all his weight lifting? That won't help matters."

"Yes!" said Veronica, her eyes lighting up. "Then if it works, he can do his duty and go straight to sleep. I won't have to listen to his boring war stories!"

Willow dug her face into Susie's shoulder, but I could still hear her muffled laughter.

"Oooh," teased Susie. "You like the soldiers do you, Veronica?"

Veronica turned to look at her. "He was a tank driver in the Royal Armoured Corps. You should see his photos. If you think he's hunky now, you should see how he looked back then!"

"I bet he was a dreamboat," I said, moving things along. "One passion and sleeping potion it is."

I took the wand I used to impress customers from behind the sales counter. "I just need to cast my circle and we can begin."

"Of course," said Veronica, facing me again.

Spinning in a circle, with the wand extended as far as I could manage in the confined space, I said a few words that people expected from witches, and invited the four earthly elements into the circle. "Okay, now we can brew the potion," I said. "The circle is cast."

Veronica watched me intently as I gathered a few herbs from the shelves and dropped them in the cauldron. "What's that?" she said, as I sprinkled a powder onto the concoction.

I added some spring water to the mix and fired up the gas stove. "Oriental pine pollen," I said. "It's very potent. It's sure to help."

Veronica looked impressed. "This is exciting," she said.

I sat down again and stirred the potion with a copper spoon, moving my face closer to the cauldron as I spoke in hushed tones. "Strong as a lion, hard as a rock, Goddess give Ron a rigid — "

Veronica gulped, and Willow and Susie shook in each other's arms, their faces bright red and tears on their cheeks.

" — libido and sleep schedule," I continued, aware of Veronica's obvious disappointment.

Veronica licked her lips. "Oh my," she said. "I can't wait to test it out."

"You be sure to tell Ron," I said. "It won't work if the person it's meant for doesn't know he's taking it. Witchcraft isn't about tricking people. Don't go slipping it into his drink without warning him."

Willow rolled her eyes at me, but I didn't take any notice, most of my customers thought witchcraft was just about spirituality — they didn't *really* expect magic to happen. I wasn't tricking anyone. Anyway, the herbs I'd used had scientifically proven effects on the human body, and I'd had some great feedback from happy customers in the past.

"I promise. Ron will be just as happy as I'll be if it works, believe me," said Veronica, with a knowing wink.

I took a small glass bottle from a shelf and pulled out the cork stopper. "Just a teaspoon or two at a time," I warned, ladling the potion into the bottle.

"You have my word," said Veronica, pulling her purse from her bag. "How much do I owe you?"

I shook my head. "Not a penny," I said, handing her the bottle. "I wouldn't dream of charging you after what Mabel put you through."

"Well, you know what they say, don't look in a horse's mouth."

"Don't look a gift horse in the mouth," I corrected.

Veronica put the potion in her bag. "Yes, that's it. Thank you, Penelope. I'm going straight back to the home now. There's a little party on tonight for the residents and their families. This potion's sure to work when Ron's had a few brandies."

Susie led Veronica off the boat as I tidied up the

shop. "Take care, Veronica," I called, as she shouted goodbye. "Enjoy the party!"

"And the after party," giggled Willow.

I raised my eyebrows. "At least their having fun. It could be worse."

"True," said Willow. She looked around the shop. "I am jealous of you, Penny. I'd love to live on a boat."

"You wouldn't be saying that if you'd been frozen in place for a week, waiting for the canal to thaw out so you could go and buy some more coal for the fire." I said, shuddering at the memory.

"I'm sure the good times outweigh the bad."

She was right of course. "Yes, I've had some wonderful experiences. Speaking of which, let's set the barbecue up on the bank, and drink wine with our feet dipped in the water." Willow's face dropped. "I'm sorry, I forgot," I said. "You can still dip them in the water though. You don't need to hide them from Susie, she's seen far worse than that since she's known our family secret."

"Far worse than what?" said Susie, stepping down into the shop.

"Granny shrank my feet," said Willow. "It was an accident, sort of. She was trying to shrink my boobs."

Susie laughed. "I'd keep them hidden for the moment," she said. "I've just seen a mop of ginger hair on a very tall man coming through the woods."

"Told you he likes you," said Willow, grinning.

"Barney likes you?" said Susie. "That's news to me."

"Me too," I said. "It's a fantasy that Willow and Granny have cooked up. Come on, let's see what he wants."

CHAPTER FIVE

*B*arney took long swaggering strides across the grass with a big smile on his face. He was still in his uniform, but I doubted it was a police related matter he was there to see me about.

His hair was quite fabulous I supposed — very ginger, and a lot of it, matching the freckles that spattered his face. His uniform was as ill-fitting as ever, with his trousers riding high on his boots, and his short shirt sleeves far too big for his thin arms. The stab proof jacket he wore looked four sizes too big, and I hid a smile as he stopped in front of me. "I hope you don't mind me popping down to see you, I just wanted to make sure that you're okay. It must be scary down here on your own."

"I'm not on my own tonight, obviously," I said, looking at Willow and Susie. "But even if I was, I'm

UNDER LOCK AND KEY

used to it. I've been moored up in the middle of nowhere on my own, and I did just fine without a policeman to look after me, thank you very much."

Barney blushed, and guilt sucker punched me. It wasn't that I didn't like Barney, it was just that I didn't want more fuel to be added to Granny and Willow's gossip fire. "Thanks for looking in on me though, and thanks for mowing the grass. I really appreciate it."

"Just trying to be helpful to the resident witch. I want to keep on your good side, I don't want to be turned into a frog or something," he joked.

"It was really kind of you, Barney," I said.

Barney looked at Susie and Willow who were in the process of lighting the barbecue, whilst obviously listening to our conversation. "Having a barbecue, huh?"

"Yes," I said. Barney's deductive police skills were on top form as always.

"Food tastes so much better when it's cooked outdoors, doesn't it?" he said, licking his lips.

"Would you like to stay for some, Barney?" said Willow, much to my annoyance. "We've got steak, burgers, and sausages."

"And salad," said Susie.

"And salad," confirmed Willow, placing some plates and cutlery on one of the tables. "If you like that sort of thing."

"I don't suppose he can," I said, turning away

from Barney so he couldn't see me scowling at my sister. "He's on duty."

"I've finished actually," he said. "I'm on standby tonight, so I can't have any of that wine," he said, as Susie opened a bottle. "But I could really tackle a steak. And maybe a sausage. Or two. And a handful of salad. Maybe a bread roll too."

"Well that settles it," said Willow. "You're staying for dinner, Barney. Would you like to cook it? I know men are better at barbecues than women, and you can't get more manly than a policeman."

Maybe Mum had been right about Willow. She did seem to be pushing her devil's dumplings out a little too far. Or maybe it was just the way she was standing — her feet were at very odd angles, and she seemed to be having trouble balancing again.

Barney slipped his stab jacket off and removed his clip-on tie, laying them on the table with his police radio next to them. I hoped that clip on ties were standard police uniform and not a reflection on Barney's dressing skills. "I'd love to cook for you ladies," he gushed, puffing his chest out.

I shrugged. "Right, well I suppose I'll have a drink. Willow would you come into the boat and help me get some of my homemade wine, please?" I said, narrowing my eyes at her.

"Of course," said Willow, smirking.

"Are you okay, Willow?" said Barney, as my sister followed me to the boat. "You're limping."

"Athlete's foot," I said. "She sweats a lot."

Barney raised his eyebrows and blushed again. "Oh, sorry to hear that, Willow. I wasn't trying to be nosy."

"Don't listen to my sister, Police Constable Dobkins," said Willow. "She's pulling your leg. I hurt myself doing gymnastics. I can get my leg right around the back of my head, and I pulled a few muscles practising last night, that's all. Shall I show you how I do it? I'll have to put some smaller shorts on, but I'm sure Penny's got some I can borrow."

Barney blushed yet again. "No, it's okay," he mumbled. "How does everyone like their steaks? Well done or rare?"

"As they come," I said. "Come on, Willow. Let's go and get that wine."

"What are you playing at?" I said, as soon as we were in the boat and out of earshot. "*Men are better at barbecues. I can get my leg behind my head.*"

Willow giggled as I followed her to the galley kitchen. "I'm just teasing him," she said. "It's obvious he likes you and you're just being a bit... bitchy to him. I was lightening the mood, and I'd stopped until you told him I had athlete's foot!"

"I was not bitchy!"

"You were."

I sighed. "I suppose I was, wasn't I?" I grabbed two bottles of wine from the rack on the counter. "You know I don't deal well with male attention, Willow. I'm not as confident as you are."

"You should be. You're beautiful, clever, and look what you've done for yourself. Not many people could make an inheritance the size Grandad left for you go this far. I'll probably waste mine when I reach twenty-one, but you own a floating shop which you live in for heaven's sake! How cool is that?"

"It is pretty cool, isn't it?" I said, looking around at the cramped but cosy surroundings. "It's not like everybody can have a different view from their kitchen window whenever they fancy a change."

"Precisely, and as for me telling Barney that men are better at barbecues... what would you prefer? Slaving over hot charcoal, or sipping wine while somebody cooks for you?"

"The latter," I smiled.

"There we are then. I just massaged his ego a little, come on, let's get back out there and see how many more times he blushes tonight!"

We giggled as I opened the double shutters that were half way along the hull on the bank-side of the boat. They doubled as a third doorway onto the *Water Witch*, and a folding set of steps allowed us to climb out of the boat. I switched the radio on, giving us some background music, and helped Willow up the steps. She'd almost perfected the wooden insoles, and negotiated the journey from the belly of the boat onto dry land almost flawlessly.

"What's so funny?" said Susie, laying on her back on the grass with a glass of wine in her hand. "I heard you laughing."

Willow sat next to her. "We were just saying how nice it was to have a man cook for us."

Barney flipped a steak, his face made even redder than normal by the heat of the coals. "Pass me some plates. You're about to find out if your trust in me was warranted."

"Everything looks lovely, Barney," I said. "Thank you."

Willow gave me an approving nod. "No salad for me, Barney. Just meat and a bread roll, please."

We sat in a semi-circle on the grass as we ate and drank. Barney had cooked the meat to perfection, and we hardly spoke as we devoured our meals, watching the colours reflecting on the water as the sun began to set.

A shy otter made an appearance on the opposite bank, but vanished as Mabel returned to the mooring and joined us on the grass, pecking at the pieces of food we'd dropped. Mabel had been quite the celebrity when the newspapers had dug their teeth into the story of the barking goose, and local people had become accustomed to spotting her on the canals and towpaths. People still found her fascinating though, and Barney spent ten minutes training her to roll over in return for a small piece of sausage.

Rosie had dared to make an appearance at one point, and sat on the roof of the boat, staring at Mabel with hatred as she ate the treats Barney offered her. I'd grabbed the last of my burger and passed it to her, stroking her as she mewled her thanks, promising her that Mabel couldn't hurt her.

Time passed quickly, and with two empty bottles of wine on the grass, and a coffee cup next to Barney, we chatted and listened to the radio in the glow of the lights from the boat. Sitting next to the *Water Witch* with the warm breeze in the trees behind me, the water lapping against the boat, and my bed a few meters away, was the reason I'd decided to live on the water, and I lay back contentedly as I listened to Barney telling us about his days' work.

"I've been trusted with a big case," he said, "Sam Hedgewick has been receiving threats. The Sergeant put me in charge. I've got to interview a few suspects tomorrow, although that's going to take some time — he seems to have rubbed a lot of people up the wrong way. He's had emails from over fifteen people."

"We heard about it," said Susie. "I was going to see if there was a story in it, but I got side-tracked taking photos of all those old cars. I only put them on my website today, and I've already got a classic car magazine asking to buy a few. They want me to cover the show too," she beamed. "I'm spending the day there tomorrow."

"He's within his rights to sell whatever properties he wants," continued Barney, acknowledging Susie's good news with a smile and a nod. "People can't just threaten him. I'll see to it that he's safe, don't you worry about that."

I smiled to myself as I imagined Sam's reaction when he found out that Barney was charged with ensuring his safety. Barney tried his best at policing, but was famous for being overpowered by one of the towns hardened criminals — Mavis Henshaw. The eighty-year-old had almost broken Barney's finger with her walking stick when he'd been called to the greengrocers to investigate reports that Mavis had been stealing lychees. Barney had been forced to call for back up, and had never fully lived the incident down.

"This is Wickford," said Willow. "I'm sure Sam Hedgewick is perfectly safe."

"Well, he's got me on his six now," boasted Barney, oblivious to our silent giggles.

"I'm sure he'll sleep well tonight," I said.

Barney's radio crackled on the table behind us. "P.C Dobkins. Come in."

Barney leapt to his feet, scaring Mabel, who gave a little whine. "Duty calls," he said grabbing his radio.

He spoke into it in a monotone voice. "PC Dobkins here."

The radio crackled again. "A body's been found. In the canal below the Lock and Key pub. We're treating it as murder."

Barney's eyes widened, and I glanced at Willow and Susie. They'd turned white.

"Do we have an ID?" said Barney, his voice cracking.

"It's Sam Hedgewick. He's been hit on the head. Get there immediately. Sergeant Cooper is waiting for you."

Barney looked at us as he put his stab jacket and tie on and clipped his radio to his belt. "Oh God," he said. "Now I'm for it. Poor Sam. I was supposed to be looking after him." His panicked face whitened and he gazed at the floor.

"Calm down," I said. "You weren't due to interview anyone until tomorrow, there's nothing you could have done tonight. You weren't his bodyguard."

"Granny said you stopped him arguing with a rough looking guy today. She actually called him a *badboy*," said Willow. "Maybe he's got something to do with it?"

"I didn't take much notice," said Barney, adjusting his stab jacket. "That was before I knew Sam was getting threats, and I was preoccupied with making sure those old cars didn't block up the roads. I can't even remember what colour hair he had!"

"Barney," I soothed. "You go now. I'll speak to Granny first thing in the morning while the memory is still fresh in her head. Go and collect evidence or whatever it is you need to do."

"I've never dealt with a murder before," said Barney. "This is new to me, and there's so many people who were angry with him."

"Go," I said. "You'll be fine."

Barney looked at us one last time, turned on the spot, and sprinted towards the footpath with Mabel hot on his heels.

"Good luck!" Susie shouted.

"Poor Barney," said Willow, as Barney vanished into the darkness and Mabel came sauntering back to us.

"Poor Sam," I said. "Barney will be fine. Sam's dead."

"Come on," said Susie. "Let's get inside the boat. I don't feel like anymore wine. We'll clear the mess up in the morning."

We trudged into the boat and made some tea, sitting at the L-shaped dinette area to drink it as we came up with theories about who could have killed Sam Hedgewick.

"Emily the florist?" said Susie. "The note in the window seemed pretty nasty."

She passed her phone to Willow so she could have a look at the photo of the note.

"Not Emily," said my sister when she'd read it. "She's too timid. And too lovely. She was just lashing out."

I brought my sister up to speed with what had happened in the allotments, and came up with my own appraisal of the situation. "Hilda Cox," I said, "most of the other allotment owners too, the badboy, and anyone else who rents a property Sam's selling. Veronica told me that Sam was a gambling man too — maybe the badboy is someone he owes money to? The police are going to have to work hard. There's so many suspects."

Susie yawned and stretched her arms above her head. "I agree," she said, "but I'm too tired to think about it now. I should be at the murder scene but I've had too much wine to drive. I'll get up early in the morning and get down there. The car show will have to wait, this is far more important. We haven't had a murder in Wickford for a long time. This is a real story."

Willow stood up. "I'm tired too. Help me make this bed, and we'll get some sleep. Susie can share your bed with you. I'd be embarrassed if my baby feet dug into you during the night."

We laughed as we collapsed the dinette table and placed the cushions on top of it to form a perfectly good double bed. "There's bedding in the storage underneath it," I said, hugging my sister. "Sleep tight."

Susie and I top and tailed in my bed, with Rosie snuggled up in the small gap between us. I'd opened the stern doors, and a warm breeze blew over us. We lay in silence listening to the night sounds until Susie tapped me on my leg. "Tell me the story of how the haven was made," she said.

"Again? Do you never get bored of the same story?"

"I like it, and anyway, you get to go there someday, I only get to hear about it. Tell it the way your mum used to tell us when we were little."

I closed my eyes. "Okay," I said. "Once upon a time, a long time ago, when people were afraid of witches, there was a very powerful witch called Maeve. She was a good witch, but one day she caught a man trying to steal the eggs from her chickens, and turned him into a toad for a day."

"Remember the face your mum used to make when she pretended to turn us into toads?" Susie said from the darkness. "It terrified us."

"Not as much as it scared Willow," I giggled. "She was only six when we were eleven."

"Go on," said Susie. "I won't interrupt again."

"Unluckily for Maeve," I continued, "somebody saw her cast the spell and reported her to the village elders. A week later the Witchfinder General arrived with his soldiers and set about building a bonfire to burn Maeve to death on. Maeve was a brave witch, and refused to use magic to stop the soldiers from burning her. She didn't want to hurt anyone, and she knew that if she did, things would become far worse for other witches, so she accepted her fate."

I laid my hand on Rosie to settle her as an owl hooted outside. "As the flames licked at the base of her robes and burned her legs, Maeve closed her eyes tight and imagined being somewhere nicer, somewhere more peaceful, a place where she wasn't in pain. Witnesses who were watching the burning said the clouds opened and a flash of lightning burst from the sky, turning Maeve into dust. They believed it was God's doing, and it gave them the encouragement they needed to carry on burning witches... except they never found another witch. Not a real one anyway."

"Because of the haven," whispered Susie.

"Yes. Maeve had accidentally managed to cast a spell so powerful it sucked most of the magic from the world and conjured up a magical dimension, a place where witches could be free from persecution. A safe haven. Back then of course, a witch could enter at any time, but when witches stopped being hunted and killed, Maeve changed the rules of entry so witches would enjoy this world before going to the haven. Now we need to prove ourselves before Maeve grants us our entry spell."

"You'll meet Maeve one day, Penny," slurred Susie as she drifted off to sleep. "How amazing is that?"

"Very," I said, and joined my friend in sleep as I listened to the water gently lapping against the hull.

CHAPTER SIX

*S*usie shook me awake. "It's seven o'clock," she said. "I'm going to the murder scene. I want to be the first journalist there. I doubt any reporters got there last night." She applied a little lipstick and put the tube in her bag. "I've fed Rosie, cleaned up the mess outside, and Willow is going to walk me up the hill to my car. Her feet have grown back and she wants to use them. She says you don't know what you've lost till they're gone."

I rubbed my eyes and yawned. "Do you want breakfast first? I bought bacon and eggs."

"No thanks. I'm kicking myself because I drank too much last night to drive. I need to go."

"Drive safe," I said, as Willow climbed the steps from the bedroom onto the stern decking.

"I will, and remember to ask Granny about that badboy. I have a feeling Barney will need some help."

I swung my feet out of bed and rubbed more sleep from my eyes. "Me and Willow will go straight to her house when we've had breakfast. I'll let you know what we find out."

I watched Willow and Susie through the window as they disappeared up the path with Mabel running ahead, scaring birds from the undergrowth.

As I waited for Willow to return, I cooked bacon and eggs, and poured us both a coffee when I heard her footsteps echoing through the boat. We ate our breakfast quickly, admired Willow's feet, and both took a shower, with Willow going first as it would take her far longer to fix her hair afterwards than it would me.

"Mum just phoned," said Willow, when I stepped out of the bathroom. "She's worried about Granny. She's not answering her phone, and she can't see her through the telescope."

Hazelwood cottage was on the top of a hill to the east of Wickford, and Granny's home, Ashwood Cottage, was on a hill to the west. With a perfect line of sight between the two highest points in the town, Mum had a telescope in her bedroom through which she spied on Granny, and Granny had a set of binoculars through which she returned the favour. Many a lie had been exposed in the past, and many an argument caused, thanks to the high-powered lenses.

"Granny will be fine," I said. "She's probably recovering from whatever that *gentleman caller* did to her with his needles. We'll go and see her as soon as I've got dressed, and find out about this badboy for Barney."

Wickford was busier than normal, and policemen and women were knocking on the doors of houses in the town centre. The Lock and Key pub, which sat on top of a small cliff directly over the canal and towpath, was cordoned off with tape, and Barney was standing next to the makeshift barrier, keeping people away. He looked tired, and gave me a small smile as I stopped the car alongside him.

"Where's Susie?" I said. As I lowered the window, her car was parked less than fifty metres away, but she was nowhere to be seen.

"They've let her down there with the other reporters," Barney said glumly, pointing at the narrow set of stone steps next to the pub which ran down to the canal. "She's at the murder scene, while I'm up here stopping nosy people from getting too close. It's not my fault Sam got murdered. I should be down there with them."

"Who says it's your fault?" said Willow, leaning over my lap to speak through the window.

"Sergeant Cooper," said Barney. "Well, he didn't actually *say* it was my fault, but considering I was given the job of investigating the threats to Sam, you'd think I'd be down there with the rest of them."

"He'll come around," I said, "anyway, we're on our way to Granny's. Maybe what she tells us about the man she saw arguing with Sam will help you. She's got a vicious eye for details."

"I remember he had tattoos," said Barney, leaning closer to the window, and lowering his voice as the onlookers watched him. "But I can't remember what they were. I can't remember how tall he was either — everyone looks short next to me. The sergeant hasn't even asked me if I know anything yet, he's too busy trying to impress the detectives from the CID."

"Don't worry," I said. "As soon as we've spoken to Granny I'll let you know what she said. I'll text you."

"Thank you," said Barney. "Hopefully the Sergeant won't ask me any questions before then. Don't go telling your Granny that I can't remember, though. If she does need to be interviewed as a witness, it will make me look silly if people find out that I couldn't even remember what a potential suspect looks like."

"Don't worry," said Willow. "We want to help you."

"Thank you," said Barney. "Both of you. I don't want to lose my job over this. I like being a policeman. I know I'm not Sherlock Holmes, but I like trying to help people."

Poor Barney. I put the car in gear and began edging away from the pavement. "I'll text you as soon as I know anything."

Barney put a hand up and waved as I watched him in the rear-view mirror.

"So, we're helping to solve a murder," said Willow, rubbing her hands together. "How exciting!"

I took the left turn that led us to the hill which Granny lived on. "I wouldn't go that far," I said. "We're just helping a friend keep his job. Anyway, the man Granny saw isn't the only suspect."

"The game is afoot!"

"The what is a what?"

"Don't you watch Sherlock?" said Willow. "Oh, of course you don't. You don't even own a television."

The narrow lane flattened out as we reached the top of the hill, and I turned right through the open wooden gates of Granny's property. The little cottage was as colourful as my mother's, with flowers blooming in the garden and a fresh coat of yellow paint on the old walls. A tall stack of fresh firewood filled the lean-to shed which was attached to one wall, and I parked the car next to it, happy that Granny was still fit enough to chop her own wood.

Granny appeared at the kitchen window, and I waved and smiled at her. She ducked quickly out of sight, her face looking panicked. Willow frowned. "What's her problem?" she said.

I opened the car door and stepped out. "I hope she hasn't had another dementia accident. That's probably why she's not answering the phone to Mum. Come on, let's see if she's okay."

The thick wooden front door was locked, which was unusual. Granny feared few things, and burglars were at the bottom of that very short list. Willow swung the heavy brass knocker into the metal mounting plate, the sound echoing over the hilltop and into the woods. "Granny," she shouted. "It's Willow and Penny! We know you're in, we saw you at the window!"

"Granny!" I echoed. "Mum's worried about you, and we've got some gossip! There's been a murder!"

"My feet are better too!" added Willow.

The window above us creaked open, and we stepped back to look up. Granny poked her head out and gazed down at us with narrowed eyes. "Good news on the feet, Willow, but a *murder*? Are you making that up just to get into my home? I'm trying to have a restful day. I don't need intrusions."

"No, honestly," I said. "Sam Hedgewick was murdered last night! Let us in and we'll tell you about it. You might be able to help, too. The man you saw arguing with Sam might be a suspect, maybe you can tell us something about him that will help solve the crime."

"Me, solve a crime? Like Mrs Doubtfire? Wait there, I'll let you in, but you're not to go in the kitchen. I'm... erm, baking a cake... using a... secret recipe. You can't go in there."

"She means Miss Marple," said Willow, as Granny slammed the window. "And I can't smell any baking."

The door creaked open an inch, and granny peered through the small gap. "It's just the two of you?" she said.

"Yes, just me and Willow," I promised. "What's wrong, Granny? You seem nervous."

"Nothing happened last night!" said Granny. "I mean, nothing's wrong, dear. Everything's just fine, and I'd stand up in a court of law and say exactly that if I was made to."

"Okay, that all sounds normal... are you going to let us in?" said Willow, glancing sideways at me.

Granny opened the door wide and stood aside to let us pass her.

"I can't smell a cake baking," I said.

"It's a secret recipe," said Granny. "If you could smell the ingredients, it wouldn't be a secret for long, would it? Now, go straight through to the lounge and tell me all about this murder."

With her back to the closed kitchen door, Granny stood and watched as we traipsed through the cottage and into the lounge. A familiar shudder ran through me as I looked at the spooky old oil paintings of our family's ancestors. They covered two walls, and the other walls were dotted with colourful modern canvases, giving the lounge the appearance of a room straggled across more than one time period.

Granny followed us in and sat in her comfy chair in front of the unlit fire, while Willow and I perched on the old sofa. "So," she said, staring at us over the rims of her glasses. "What's the gossip?"

We told her what we knew about the death of Sam Hedgewick, leaving out any mention of Barney's concerns. Granny ummed and aahed as the story unfolded, and her face lit up when we asked her to describe the so called badboy she'd seen.

"I knew my memory would come in handy one day," she said, settling further into her seat. "Now, let me think."

She closed her eyes and scrunched up her face, deep in thought. After what seemed like an eternity she snapped her eyes open. "Do you need to write it down?" she asked.

"No, we'll remember," I said.

"Okay. Six foot tall. Close cropped sand coloured hair. Wet sand mind, not dry sand. White t-shirt with a small black logo on the left side of the chest. White trainers with three red stripes, slightly dirty but certainly not old — this cat cared about how he looked — he wouldn't be seen dead in old shoes."

I bit my lip, and Willow shook against my thigh as she tried not to laugh. "Cat?" I said.

"You're too young to appreciate a cat," said Granny. "Your grandad was one though — he was the coolest cat in Wickford. Anyway, I digress. Faded denim jeans — blue. Tattoos on both arms. A dragon on the left forearm and a phoenix on the right. Both in black ink and leading beneath his t-shirt sleeves. Come to bed blue eyes, and muscles like a US Navy Seal."

"Navy Seal?" said Willow.

"American special forces, dear. Very well built gentlemen. No wedding ring — I noticed that first. In fact, no jewellery whatsoever, he's not the type to adorn himself with bling." She closed her eyes again for a second or two. "That's all I can tell you. I'm sorry I can't remember more."

Willow gulped. "That should be enough to go on," she said.

"Anyway, why do you girls want to know about him? Don't you go trying to capture him, like I said yesterday, he's a badboy."

"It's just in case we see him around," I said. "We could tell the police."

"You can tell the police that Sam was coming out

of the lawyer's office too. That's suspicious. A man visits a lawyer in the day, and he's dead that very night."

"A lawyer's office?" said Willow.

Granny sighed. "You girls need to clean your ears out. I told you yesterday, Sam was coming out of the lawyer's office when he was accosted, then that police friend of yours came along, Penelope. I don't know why you're asking me for a description anyway. Ask Barney, with his keen police mind he'll have noticed plenty of things I missed."

"Yes," I said, ignoring Willow's chuckles. "I'm sure he's already hunting him down. There's nothing suspicious about Sam going to a lawyer though. He was selling all his properties. That's the sort of thing lawyers help people with."

"Just something to bear in mind," said Granny. "Leave no stone unturned."

"I'll mention it to Barney," I said. "Anyway, Granny, how did your acupuncture go last night? Do you feel any better?"

Granny's face whitened. "It was a load of rubbish," she said. "Not worth the money I paid for it. Nothing happened here last night though! I can assure you both of that!"

"Granny," I said. "What happened here last night?"

"As I've made abundantly clear — nothing happened here last night!"

"Granny, are you crying?" said Willow.

"Curse the thought!" spat Granny, wiping her eyes with the hem of her apron. "I haven't cried since Norman died. Rest his soul. And I only cried then because your mother did the catering for the wake. I don't know what she was thinking, but everyone knows you don't trick a vegetarian into eating a ham sandwich. Those people are vicious if they find out they've ingested meat. The vicar is adamant he won't let our family ever use the hall again."

"You'd tell us if something was wrong, wouldn't you?" I said.

Granny leaned forward in her seat. "Penelope, you've known me for twenty-three years. When have I ever lied to — "

A huge crashing sound from the kitchen made Granny jump, cutting off her sentence.

"What on earth was that?" said Willow. "Is someone here?"

"Nothing happened here last night!" sobbed Granny, rocking in her seat with her arms wrapped tightly around herself. "Nothing happened here last night!"

"I'm having a look in the kitchen, Granny," I said. "I don't care what you say."

"She can't hear you," Willow said. "She looks like

one of those Vietnam veterans. You know, with the thousand-yard stare?"

I waved a hand in front of Granny's glazed eyes, but she didn't blink. "Nothing happened here last night," she mumbled, squeezing herself tighter.

"She's okay," I said. "She's just shut down for a while, like the time she discovered that the wrestling on TV was staged. She'll be fine in a few minutes."

Another loud bang from the kitchen drew our attention, and I followed Willow as she made her way down the hallway. She paused as she reached the kitchen door. "Do you think it's safe to go in?"

"It's not an intruder, otherwise Granny wouldn't have been trying to hide something. Go on, open the door."

Willow opened the door slowly, and we stared at the sight before us in disbelief. "Oh heavens," whispered Willow. "What's she done now?"

CHAPTER SEVEN

Boris the goat turned towards us as we entered the kitchen. He lowered his front hooves from the kitchen counter on which he'd been trying to tear open a packet of biscuits, and tilted his head. Pots and pans surrounded him, and another one fell from one of the open cupboards behind him. "Baa?" he said.

"Pardon?" I said, squeezing Willow's hand which she'd placed in mine.

"Maa?" he said.

"He sounds like a man." whispered Willow.

"Hello, Boris," I said, releasing Willow's hand, and taking a step towards the goat. "What are you doing in Granny's kitchen?"

Boris looked around at the mess he'd made. "Bleat?"

"Oh my goddess!" shrieked Willow. "Look at the pantry!"

The pantry door was ajar, and I took a step back as I followed Willow's frightened gaze. A man's hand hung from the gap, and the toe of a shoe prevented the door from closing fully. "Get a knife!" I said. "I'll phone the police!"

I fumbled for my phone as Willow opened a drawer and grabbed a large carving knife, which she held in front of her with both hands. "Quick," she said. "Phone someone!"

Boris took a step towards us and coughed. "There's no need for police involvement, young ladies," he said in a well-spoken upper class English accent. "Allow me to introduce myself. I'm Charleston Huang, certified member of The British Acupuncture Accreditation Board. You're perfectly safe. The man in the cupboard is me... well, to be more precise, it's the mind of this perfectly lovely creature, in my body."

"What is going on?" whispered Willow, dropping the knife a fraction. "Boris is talking to us."

Boris cleared his throat. "I could attempt to explain the not unwelcome predicament I find myself in, but I feel that Gladys would be best placed to enlighten you."

"Gladys? Granny lets you call her Gladys?" said

Willow. "Only her enemies call her Gladys, and her very good friends."

"I'm certainly not the former," said Boris. "It would be a privilege, however, to be considered the latter." Boris gazed between his front legs, attempting to look beneath his body. A bald patch above his tail was the only evidence that he'd recently been attacked by an enchanted lawnmower. "Tell me, young ladies," he said, attempting to crane his neck further under his belly. "Do I need milking?"

"No," said Willow. "You're male."

The goat lowered his voice. "Splendid. Although Gladys is a remarkable woman, I really wouldn't have felt comfortable with her interfering with me in that way."

Footsteps sounded behind us. "So, you've discovered my awful secret," said Granny. "I knew it would only be a matter of time before you pesky kids found me out."

"In all fairness, Gladys," said Boris. "The incident only happened last night. It can hardly be referred to as a matter of time. It's barely been twelve hours."

"True dat," said Granny, raising a smile from Willow even as she held a knife defensively in front of her. Granny really had to stop reading Willow's books.

"Drop the weapon, Willow," said Granny. "I'll make us all a nice cup of tea and –"

"I'm not a big fan of tea, Gladys," said Boris. "Maybe a saucer full of that delightful brandy you gave me last night."

"You gave brandy to a goat?" I said.

"He was still in his human body," said Granny. "Anyway, brandy won't harm him now. He's protected by magic. He can drink brandy all day long if he likes."

"That makes my situation sound all the more acceptable," said Boris.

"You like being a goat, Charleston?" said Willow, placing the knife back in the drawer and filling the kettle.

"It's the calmest I've felt for a long time, and please, call me Boris. If I'm to occupy this grand old beast's body, the least I can do is honour his name."

"What about *actual* Boris though?" I said. "Is he happy in your body? And why on earth is he just standing in the cupboard, is he traumatised?"

Granny opened the brandy and poured a generous glug into a saucer, laying it on the floor in front of Boris. "He's in a form of stasis. He's oblivious to what's going on and he can't move. No harm will come to him, and neither he or the goat will age until I can sort this terrible mess out."

"For the record," said Boris. "I don't consider this a mess. Life has been getting to me recently. I have no loved ones to go home to, and the relief I felt when

Gladys texted all my customers to cancel their acupuncture appointments was wholly liberating. I'm perfectly content with the surprising direction my life has taken."

Willow took a few tentative steps towards the pantry. "Can I have a look?" she said.

"I have no objections," said Boris, "but please excuse the look on my body's face. It was quite the shock to be on the receiving end of magic, although I've long believed that witches were real. Tell me, are you two young ladies witches too?"

"They try to be," said Granny.

"We are," said Willow, opening the pantry door.

I joined Willow and studied the man in the cupboard. He was thin and nearing sixty, I guessed, and obviously of Chinese heritage. His eyes were wide open, and his mouth formed a perfect o shape. He certainly seemed shocked.

"He can't stay in there until your dementia gets better, Granny," I said. "For a start, I can't reach the cakes, he's blocking the shelves."

"And he'll smell of spices," said Willow.

"You two can help me drag him upstairs before you leave. We'll put him in the guest bed." She looked at Boris who was happily lapping up brandy. "If you have no objections, Boris?"

Boris licked his lips. "I'm sure the guest bed will be the perfect place for my body to rest. I have no objections. I only wish I could help you carry me up the stairs."

I took a step out of the kitchen to gather my thoughts and send a text to Barney, listing as much of Granny's information as I could recall, remembering to tell him about the lawyer. When I re-entered the room, Willow was sitting at the table with Granny, and a cup of tea was waiting for me. They'd cleared away most of the mess Boris had made, and Granny was beginning to explain the previous night's occurrences.

"But how exactly did it happen?" asked Willow.

"Charleston, sorry *Boris,*" Granny said, smiling at the goat, "did wonders for my back. The needles didn't help my magic, but I feel twenty years younger."

Boris agreed. "She's been chopping wood since two o'clock in the morning."

"Why?" I said, sitting down.

"To hide his car under," Granny beamed. "It's in the lean to. You two didn't see it, did you? So, all that chopping was worth it."

"Don't blame your grandmother for what happened," said Boris. "I offered to relieve the goat's suffering."

"What?" said Willow.

"Boris was limping a little... after the lawnmower incident," said Granny. "Charlest — Boris, offered to help him with acupuncture. I didn't know there was residual magic from the mower left in the goat. It arced with the needles, and they swapped places."

Boris nodded, brandy dripping from the long white hairs beneath his chin. "And when Gladys tried to return us to our rightful bodies, which was quite the task — I've never seem my body move so fast, or eat grass — something happened which froze my body."

"Dementia," mumbled Granny, wiping her eyes. "And now they're stuck until I get better."

Boris laid a hoof on Granny's back, patting her gently. "There, there, Gladys. There's an old Chinese proverb — *coming events cast their shadow before them* — I knew there was something magical about you, I've always been very spiritual, you see, but I insisted on treating you and this goat. It's my fault as much as yours."

"Thank you, Boris," said Granny, patting the goats head. "That means a lot to me."

"Excuse me for saying, Boris," said Willow, "but you don't sound very Chinese."

"Willow!" snapped Granny, "you can't say things like that — it's racist!"

Boris chuckled. "Nonsense," he said. "It's a perfectly acceptable question, Gladys, and one I'd be happy to answer. My parents never left Britain, and I've only stepped foot in China once. I went to see the great wall, to please my grandfather. It was an underwhelming experience, and the *Chinese* Chinese food was very disappointing. I'm from a wealthy family, and benefitted from an Oxford education. I've led a privileged life, and it seems that life has still more surprises planned for me."

"A wise old goat," said Granny. She slammed her hand down on the table. "And don't you two go saying anything about this to that daughter of mine," she warned. "Or my wrath will be swift and fearsome."

"I agree with Gladys," said Boris, "although watching her sobbing in the garden last night casts some doubt on her claims of fearsomeness. I'm happy as I am, young ladies. Let's keep it between the four of us and my body. I'm more than happy to live as I am and play the part of a garden goat whenever you have visitors, Gladys. It will be quite invigorating."

My phone beeped. It was a message from Susie.

Poor Sam. Meet me when you can. I'll tell you what's happened x

I replied.

Meet us at Mum's cottage. We're on our way x

"We need to go, Granny." I said, showing Willow

the message. "Come on, let's get Charleston up the stairs."

Boris tapped the floor with his hoof. "Would somebody be so kind as to top my saucer up with brandy, and pass me one or two biscuits before you begin the job of hiding my body?"

CHAPTER EIGHT

Willow picked at her torn fingernail. "He didn't look like he'd be that heavy."

"At least he's safe, and tucked up under that duvet he'll be fine until Granny can switch them back," I said.

Susie's car was already outside Mum's house when we arrived. Nobody was downstairs, but Susie's and Mum's voices were coming from upstairs.

"Hello!" I shouted. "We're here." Susie came running down the stairs. "What were you doing up there?" I said.

"I was telling her about Sam, and looking through the telescope with her. She's worried about Granny, and I don't blame her. We just saw her going for a walk into the woods with Boris, and the goat looked wobbly on his feet — almost like he was drunk. Is everything okay over there?"

We sat at the kitchen table and quickly told Susie what had happened.

"Don't tell Mum," warned Willow, as Susie rocked with laughter. "Boris and Granny are happy, and Mum already thinks Granny's got a problem with animal cruelty. There's the thing with Mabel, the chicken laying ostrich eggs, Boris and the lawnmower, and now this."

Susie closed an imaginary zipper over her mouth. "My lips are sealed, a bit like that lawyer you told Barney to go and see."

"Barney's been there already?" said Willow.

"I was with him when he got Penny's text. He went straight to the lawyer's office but was only in there for five minutes. The lawyer said he had information that may be relevant to the investigation, but he had to honour his client's confidentiality. The police need to get a court order to make him hand over the information. Barney does seem a bit more relaxed since he got the text, though. He's still worried about getting in trouble of course. He just needs a break in the case to get on his Sergeant's good side again."

"Maybe we can help him," I said. "What's been happening? What do the police know about what happened to Sam?"

Susie took her camera from her bag and turned the screen towards me and Willow. "You're not squeamish, are you?"

We both shook our heads, having a family like ours had knocked any squeamishness out of us years ago.

"They pulled Sam out of the canal in the early hours of the morning, but left him on the towpath until forensics could have a look at him," said Susie.

The photo Susie showed us was of Sam laying on the towpath, wearing a suit. His visible skin was white and wrinkled but there was no blood to be seen.

"He looks like he drowned," Willow said. "He almost looks peaceful."

Susie showed us another picture. This one displayed the rear of Sam's head as a man in protective clothing and a mask examined him. "I wasn't supposed to take these photos," she said, "But they hadn't put a tent around his body when I arrived, and I managed to snap a few from half way up the steps that lead down to the towpath."

We looked at the next picture. Susie had zoomed in on Sam's head, and it didn't take a pathologist to work out the cause of death. A long wound ran along the back of his skull, and his wet hair stuck to the shape of the gash, making it simple to deduce that the murder weapon had been cylindrical.

"They found one of those things on the towpath,"

said Susie. "What do you call them, the metal tools boat owners use to open lock gates?"

"A windlass," I said.

The Wickford lock was only a few hundred metres from where Sam's body had been found, and it wasn't uncommon for boat owners to forget to stow their windlasses after passing through the gates. The canal was only wide enough for one boat for almost half a mile from where Sam had been found. Maybe it had fallen off a boat, and the murderer had found it and used it as an impromptu weapon.

"They've sent it off for forensic tests," Susie said. "And they're sending Sam for a post-mortem. The police say it will take a week for the results to come back."

"Any witnesses?" said Willow. "The Lock and Key pub balcony is right above the towpath."

"No. the police think he was murdered further along the path, near where they found the windlass, and the wind blew his body as far as the pub. There were a few boats moored up where the canal widens, but the residents were all asleep."

"How was he found?" I said. "Nobody walks along the towpath at that time of night. It was almost midnight when Barney got the radio message."

Susie put her camera away. "The Lock and Key closed at half eleven, but one guy needed to relieve himself. He went down the steps at the side of the pub to use the towpath, and saw Sam. He was still floating slowly towards the lock, so he used a tree branch to snag him, and phoned the police."

"What was Sam doing down there?" Willow said. "He doesn't strike me as the type to take moonlit walks."

"He'd been to the nursing home. Remember Veronica told us they were having a party for the residents and their families?"

We nodded.

"Well, Sam's dad's a resident there," Susie said. "He drank too much to drive home, and with Wickford being so small there were no taxis running that late. He decided to walk home, and he was murdered on his way."

"Have any suspects been arrested?" said Willow.

"The police have visited nearly twenty people, including Hilda Cox from the allotment, and Emily the florist. Most of them have watertight alibis, but they're bringing in a few of them for further questioning," said Susie. "Barney seems to think it's very important to find the guy who was arguing with Sam, and to get the lawyer to talk. He wants the lawyer's information before the police get the warrant. He thinks it will save his job."

"We can keep an eye out for Granny's badboy," I said, "but we can't make the lawyer talk."

Willow tapped the table absentmindedly. "Maybe we can," she said.

"How?" said Susie, "are you going to use your feminine charms on him?"

Willow rolled her eyes. "I was thinking more of Granny's spell book, she keeps it hidden in the cellar."

"Yes, and the doors have got more locks on it than Fort Knox," I said. "Granny will never let us use it. She calls it her weapon of mutually assured destruction. She brought it back from the haven to defend herself from attacks from other witches, back when she was a survivalist. We've got no hope of getting any help from her."

Willow smirked. "We *didn't* have any hope of getting her help, but that was before we found out about Boris. I think we've got a goat shaped ace up our sleeve. She'd hate for anyone to find out what she's done."

"We won't be able to make the spells work," I said. "Especially the ones which control people. It's old magic. We've never used it before."

"We can try," said Willow. "Otherwise that lawyer's never going to talk before Barney can redeem himself."

"Okay," I said. "We'll go back to Granny's. You can come too if you want, Susie. You can meet Charleston."

"Boris," corrected Willow.

"I'd love to come," said Susie, "but I need to edit a story I wrote about the murder. Say hello to Granny for me, though."

"What are you saying about your grandmother?" said Mum, hurrying into the kitchen, an imprint from the telescope around her eye. "She's up to something. I know it. I just saw her taking Boris into her house. I'm going straight over there to find out why she's been ignoring my calls. Was she acting strangely when you two were there?"

"Boris is recovering," Willow said quickly. "That's why Granny's taken him indoors."

Mum narrowed her eyes. "Recovering?"

Willow nodded. "That man who came last night to do acupuncture really helped Granny with her back pain."

"Not her spells though," I added.

"No, not her dementia," continued Willow. "He offered to do some acupuncture on Boris – he was limping after the lawnmower incident."

"Acupuncture on a goat?" said Mum, frowning. "Are you sure?"

"Absolutely," said Willow. "Granny just wants him to be comfortable after his ordeal. She feels guilty, so she brought him indoors."

Mum sat down at the table with us. "She should feel guilty. That poor goat. It does explain why Susie and I saw him wobbling through the woods though.

Poor thing. I still think I should drive over there and check on her."

"I was going to ask if I could borrow your car for the rest of the day," I said. "We need to go back to Granny's... Willow left her..."

"I left my phone there," said Willow, pushing her phone deeper into her pocket. "We'll make sure she's okay."

Mum shook her head slowly and sucked her bottom lip into her mouth. Her disappointed face. "I knew you'd regret buying that boat with your inheritance. Don't you feel silly now? Having to borrow my car when you could have bought two of your own?"

"I don't regret it," I said. "I don't want a car."

"You could have fooled me," said Mum. She turned to look at Willow. "Treat this as a lesson, Willow. When you reach twenty-one and get your money, don't go spending it on something as ridiculous as your sister did. Use it wisely."

Willow's face reddened. "I don't think she wasted it, and neither does Granny — and it was *her* husband's money. Penelope owns a business, and she's happy. How can that be a waste?"

Mum sighed, ignoring Willow's spirited interjection. "I just think you could have got a real job Penelope." She gazed across the table at Susie with a big smile on her face. "Like Susie has. She makes a difference to people's lives when they read her stories.

Did she tell you she's sold a story about the murder to The Herald? That's something to be proud of."

"No I haven't told them yet, Maggie," said Susie. "I was just about to when you came in."

"Susie couldn't wait to tell me when she got here," said Mum, "and I don't blame her. What a stroke of genius she had for the title of the story." She patted Susie on the hand. "Tell them, sweetheart."

Susie gave me a pained expression. I gave her a smile. "Go on," I said. "I'd love to know."

"It's not as brilliant as your mum is making out," said Susie. "I've called it *Murder under Lock and Key.*"

Mum let out a low whistle of admiration. "Because Sam was murdered and his body was found below the Lock and Key pub, the term lock and key can also mean somethi — "

"We get it, Mum," said Willow. "Well done, Susie!"

"It's a shame that a man being murdered was the break I needed to sell a big story," said Susie.

"That's life," said Mum. "Anyway, you can use my car again, girls. I'll go to the haven to visit Aunt Eva and pick up some ingredients for a lasagne. Tell my mother I'll pop over and see her tomorrow."

"We will," I said, "and tell Aunt Eva we said hello."

CHAPTER NINE

"Not you two again," said Granny as we walked into her kitchen. She'd reverted to leaving the front door unlocked again, and everything seemed normal, apart from the fact that somewhere on her property was a talking goat. Granny was studying a recipe book, and closed it as we sat at the table next to her. "Two visits in one day, to what do I owe the pleasure?"

"Where's Boris?" said Willow.

"He's in the lounge watching TV. *Antiques Roadshow* was on when I left him, he's relaxing a little before his bath."

"You're bathing him?" said Willow.

"It's either that or he lives in the garden. He's very cultured, but he does stink a little."

"That's nice," said Willow sarcastically. "Magic his mind into the body of a goat, and then threaten him with living in the garden. How very *tolerant* of you."

Granny shrugged. "He knows he smells. I've seen him sniffing his leg pits. He'll be happier when he smells of lavender bubble bath." Granny wrinkled her forehead into a frown. "Anyway, what are you two doing back here? Something tells me you haven't come to check on me and Boris."

I looked at Willow, and she gave me an almost imperceptible nod. She wanted me to ask Granny. I licked my lips. "It's simple," I said, "we haven't told Mum about what you did to Boris, and it will remain that way if you agree to help us."

Granny's frown deepened. "I don't like where this is going," she said. "This is the sort of thing people say in films before they blackmail somebody. You'd better not try and blackmail me, because if you do, my wrath will be swift and — "

"Fearsome," interrupted Willow. "Yes. We know. But not as fearsome as Mum's wrath will be if she finds out what you did to Charleston Huang, and imagine what your friends in the haven would say when the word got around. You'll be a laughing stock when you finally remember your entry spell."

Granny scrunched up her face and prepared to

click her fingers. "Think about it before you cast it," I warned. "You're already hiding a talking goat, and you don't want to be responsible for something bad happening to me and Willow, do you? Mum would never forgive you."

Granny sighed and lowered her hand, sparks still arcing between her fingertips. "What help do you need that requires these levels of manipulation?"

"We need your spell book," I said.

"You can kiss my wrinkly old a — "

"Or we'll tell Mum about Boris," threatened Willow.

Granny nibbled her bottom lip. "Why do you want my spell book?"

"We want to help find out who killed Sam Hedgewick," I said.

"And help Barney," Willow said. "He was in charge of finding out who was threatening Sam."

"And Sam died on his watch," pondered Granny, "add that to the fact that you've got a thing for him, Penelope, and I can begin to see why you think my magic can help you."

"I don't have a thing for Barn — "

Granny waved me quiet. "How exactly do you think my spell book can help?"

"We need to get information out of somebody," I said. "The lawyer you said Sam had been in to see.

He's got information that could help Barney, but he's not talking — client confidentiality, apparently."

Granny nodded. "And you want to make him sing like a canary."

"Something like that," said Willow.

Granny closed her eyes and took a deep breath. "I can't give you that book," she said, snapping her eyes open. "You two don't have the experience to use the spells."

Willow spoke slowly and clearly, moving her face closer to Granny's. "Imagine if Mum ever did find out about Boris... but then you told her *you'd* been helping us learn more magic. Just picture how happy she'd be that you were helping us to ascend to the haven. She'd forget about Boris in an instant."

Granny closed her eyes again briefly. "I'll do it, but I'll only show you how to use one spell. You girls will have to work out the rest of them yourselves, and you must promise that no one will be turned into a toad."

"That spell's in the book?" said Willow.

"There's better than that in there," she said. "I compiled that book using old spells from the haven when I had that... funny few months."

"When you became a survivalist?" I said.

"I prefer the term prepper," said Granny. "There was a lot of friction in the haven at the time, the voodoo witches from Haiti were fighting with the Scottish witches, and I was afraid it would spill into this world. I wanted to protect my family. You two included. It went to my head a little, that's all."

"It took a long time to eat all those tins of food in your cellar afterwards, didn't it Granny?" said Willow.

Granny stood up. "Yes. I'll never look at another tin of corned beef again. Or peaches." She shook her head. "I don't like to talk about those days. I'll go to the cellar and get that book for you on one condition."

"Yes?" said Willow.

"The old tin bath I used to use for your mother and uncle is tucked away in the back of the pantry. Get it out and fill it with hot water and bubble bath. You can help me bath Boris, and then I'll teach you how to cast one of my spells."

Boris stepped calmly into the bath. "It's not as if I'm undressed, is it?" he said, "because I don't want any of you to get the idea that I'd normally allow myself to be bathed by three members of the opposite sex. My days in Oxford were heady, but even then, I never came close to doing anything like that."

"Just enjoy it" said Granny. "I've used lavender bubble bath. It's calming."

"I've never felt calmer," said Boris. He lowered himself to his knees in the suds. "Help me onto my back, would you?"

Willow and Granny helped flip him over, and I placed a rolled-up towel under the back of his head to protect him from the thin rim of the bath. Only his four outstretched legs and his horned head were visible above the bubbles as he settled down, and he closed his eyes as we began massaging his matted white hair.

"You seem very natural as a goat," said Willow. "You're taking it all very well."

"Willow," said Granny. "We treat Boris as if he has always been a goat. He's trans-species. It's transphobic and intolerant of you to allude to his time as a human. Boris wants to be a goat, and we will afford him that courtesy."

"Calm down, Gladys," said Boris. "I'm really not offended. Why don't you go and sit in the lounge and let me get to know your grandchildren? You deserve a rest. You must be aching after chopping all that wood."

"I do deserve a rest, don't I?" said Granny, her knees clicking as she stood up. "Make sure his head doesn't slip under the water, girls, and just shout if you need anything, Boris. I found another bottle of brandy in the cellar alongside the spell book and an old tin of corned beef, just let me know when you're ready for a dram or two."

"She's a wonderful woman," said Boris, when Granny had left the kitchen. "But she seems very preoccupied with race and suchlike. I've heard her call three people on the TV racist today, and she refused to join me in watching *Antiques Roadshow* because somebody brought in an old Aboriginal boomerang to be valued. She began ranting about colonialism and cultural appropriation. It was quite unnerving."

I lowered my voice — Granny still had very good hearing. "She used to be an SJW," I said. "She's still holding on to some of the values."

"A social justice warrior?" said Boris. "How interesting."

"No," said Willow. "Not a social justice warrior. It was far worse than that. She was a social justice witch."

"My interest is piqued," said Boris, sighing as Willow applied shampoo to his head. "Tell me more."

"Has she told you about the haven?" I said.

"Oh yes, and it sounds such a magical and lovely place."

I passed Willow a loofah which she used to scrub behind the goat's ears. "It's not always lovely there," I said, "there's witches and warlocks in the haven from all parts of this world, and they don't always see eye-to-eye."

"Especially the Copper Haired Wizard of the west," said Willow. "Mum and Granny say he's always stirring up unrest."

"He sounds fabulous," said Boris.

"He is to his followers," I said, "but a few years ago, he decided he wanted to deport all the Haitian voodoo witches from his lands."

"And then conjure up a wall of spells around their lands to keep them inside," added Willow.

"Fascinating," murmured Boris, his rear left leg twitching as I scrubbed it.

I continued. "A few of the witches, including Granny, wanted to help the Haitians. They decided that the Copper Haired Wizard was evil, and set about defending the rights of the voodoo witches. Granny picked up a few tips from the protestors she saw on the news in this world, and before Mum and my Aunt Eva could stop her, she was the leader of a group called the Social Justice Witches."

"The group got carried away," said Willow. "When the Copper Haired Wizard capitulated to the SJW's and agreed to tear down the wall, they turned their attention to gay and lesbian witch rights, and it spiralled out of control from there."

"Your grandmother sounds like a real firebrand," said Boris.

"Oh, she is," I said. "Too much for the haven though. When she burnt down a centuries old magical rose bush, claiming that women who made love potions from the petals were demeaning themselves by needing the forced affection of a man, Maeve banished her from the haven for a year. Her blue hair is the only physical reminder of the time, but if you look closely at her nose, you can still see where her piercings went."

"I knew she was a vibrant woman when I arrived yesterday," said Boris. "Although I had no idea just how vibrant." Boris went suddenly rigid, and spun his head towards the kitchen window, his ears splashing water across the floor, and his curled horns barely missing my fingers. "There's a car coming through the gates. Are we expecting company?"

"No," said Willow, standing up to look through the window. "It's a police car," she said, craning her neck. "It's Barney and Sergeant Cooper."

Granny came running into the kitchen, flapping her arms around her head and making loud panting sounds. "It's the feds! They must know Charleston's gone missing! I can't spend one more night in the big house – I'll be someone's bitch within the hour! If they find his car, or him in the guest bed, it's all over for me!"

"Granny," I said grabbing her wrist. "Calm down, they're probably here because Barney admitted to

Sergeant Cooper that you have a better description of that badboy."

"Boris," said Granny, snatching her wrist from my grip. "You won't give the game away, will you? You'll stay in character as a goat?"

"Gladys," said Boris, blowing bubbles from his nostrils. "You have my word. Although I can assure you that no one knew I was coming here, and I have nobody in my life who would have even noticed I'd vanished."

Granny breathed more easily. "Well, I'm torching your car as soon as I get the chance! I can't have that sort of evidence right next to my cottage!"

"We can't let them see Boris in the bath," said Willow. "It's not normal!"

"Of course it's normal," said Granny. "He's just a goat and we're bathing him. I'm sure they've seen far more interesting things in their line of work. Anyway, I'm not inviting them in unless they show me a warrant. They can conduct their business on my doorstep."

"Penelope," said Boris, as Granny scampered off to open the door. "Gladys just hinted that she'd been to prison. For what crime, may I enquire?"

"She spent three hours in a cell in Wickford police station," laughed Willow. "With the door open and as much tea as she could drink."

"She was arrested while she was still in social

justice witch mode, after being banished from the haven." I said. "She threw eggs at the Police Superintendent and told him he was part of the patriarchy which was oppressing her. Using less pleasant language than that, though."

I joined Willow at the window and watched Granny talking to Barney and the Sergeant as she guided them back down her pathway and towards their car. Barney dwarfed Sergeant Cooper — although that wasn't hard — the sweating red-faced law keeper was almost as short as Granny, and he would have looked far more at home in a pudding baker's apron than a policeman's uniform. He scratched notes in his book as Granny spoke to him, and shook his head periodically at Barney, who gazed at his feet, looking embarrassed.

"What's happening?" said Boris.

"I think Sergeant Cooper found out that Barney needed Granny's help," murmured Willow. "Barney looks very ashamed."

Finally, Sergeant Cooper slammed his notebook closed and he and Barney got back into the car and drove away as Granny made her way back into the cottage. "Right," she said, scowling as she walked into the kitchen. "Let's teach you how to use my spell book. That horrible little man was awful to Barney. That ginger simpleton needs our help."

I took a sharp intake of breath. "Granny!" I scolded. "That's an awful thing to say!"

"Not my words, dear," she said. "That's what his Sergeant called him. You need to get that lawyer to talk, and you need to make him tell Barney what he knows. I'd like to see that smug look wiped off that Sergeant's face. Barney needs to help solve Sam's murder."

CHAPTER TEN

After helping Granny dry Boris off, and learning how to cast one of the spells in the book, Willow and I headed back to my boat with the tome of spells.

Mabel was nowhere to be seen, and Rosie was sunbathing on the roof. She leapt off when she saw us coming and scampered inside — no doubt attempting to trick me into filling her bowls again. A colourful narrowboat chugged past on the canal, and Willow and I both waved back at the elderly couple who shared the steering duties at the rear.

I handed Rosie a fish shaped treat, explaining to the overweight cat that I knew Susie had already fed her. Willow placed the big book of spells on the dinette table and opened it at the index. The musty smell of the old paper reminded me of the books

Mum used to read to me when I was little, and I joined Willow in searching for the best spell to help make the lawyer give us the information Barney needed.

Granny had spent twenty minutes teaching me how to cast one of the simplest spells in the book, and my head still hurt from the effort. I'd finally managed to make the chair float half an inch above the floor, and Boris had slammed his hooves together in an excited and dangerous attempt at applause.

"What sort of spell are we looking for?" said Willow, running her long fingernail down the eclectic list of spells which were neatly written in black ink.

"I'm not sure," I said. "A truthfulness spell?"

"I don't think so," said Willow. "A truthfulness spell would probably be best for somebody who was lying. The lawyer's not lying — he's just refusing to talk."

"A spell of persuasion?" I suggested.

Willow flipped the page and ran her finger down the spells beginning with the letter P. "Here we are," she said. "Page two hundred and ten."

Willow leafed through the pages until she found the spell we were looking for. "It looks complicated," I said.

"Remember what Granny said," urged Willow. "Think the spell, and then sip the magic from the air like a fine wine."

The symbols and letters that were the spell, made little sense. A triangle here, a cross there, the number nine next to the letter W — but as I silently read the two lines of symbols over and over again, the same swelling feeling in my head occurred as it had when granny had taught me to cast the levitation spell. "Something's happening," I said. "My head hurts."

"Granny said that will pass as you get better at them," said Willow. "Have you got milk in the fridge?"

"Yes," I said. "Why? Have you suddenly developed a liking for it?"

Willow hated milk. She'd hated it since she'd been a baby, and Mum had been forced to feed her sweetened condensed milk — the type that came in a tin. Willow blamed those early days on the sweet tooth that she still needed to placate on a regular basis.

"No. I still hate it, but why don't you try and persuade me to drink some?"

I smiled, and studied the spell again. If I could get Willow to drink milk, I could persuade anybody to do anything. I skim read the symbols over and over, my eyes crisscrossing the page, and my head pounding the same way it did when I drank too much elderberry wine. Granny had assured me that the pain in my head was the spell imprinting itself on me, and when it had seared itself permanently in my mind, I'd be able to access it just by thinking about it. As she'd explained, her dementia problems were due to her thinking about one spell, but another being taken from her mind's muddled filing cabinet.

Willow put a hand on mine. "Remember what she said — when you're ready to cast it, taste the magic in the air and think hard about what you want to happen. Then click your fingers."

I closed my eyes and sucked a small amount of air between my teeth. Granny had said you could taste the magic, but all I could taste was the overpowering flavour of Rosie's tuna flavoured breakfast which permeated the living area. I licked my lips, concentrating on what I wanted Willow to do, and sucked in a little more air. The distinct flavour of metal filled my mouth — reminding me of the taste of a penny piece. Not that I often sucked on copper currency, but it was the flavour that came to mind nonetheless. I clicked my fingers, and the tips tingled with static electricity.

The cushion I was sharing with Willow settled a little as she stood up, and I opened my eyes to watch.

She looked at me with shock on her face, and began walking slowly towards the fridge. "This is weird," she said, opening the fridge door. "I know I don't want to be doing this, but I have to."

I concentrated harder. Willing my sister to drink some milk. She reached into the fridge and retrieved the carton, unfolding the spout, and lifting it to her face. She took a long swallow and looked at me in horror as she began gagging. I immediately stopped the persuasive thoughts, and Willow hurried to the sink, coughing and spluttering as she spat milk down the plug hole. She turned the tap on and shovelled handfuls of water into her mouth. "That was disgusting. I'll never understand why people willingly drink milk," she gasped. "Apart from in tea. With sugar."

"How did it feel?" I said.

Willow scooped more water into her mouth and wiped her lips on a tea towel as Rosie watched her curiously. "It was strange," she said. "It was like the feeling I get when I know I've eaten too much chocolate, but there's still some left in the box. I know I shouldn't, but I have to eat it. The lawyers got no chance if you can pull that off again!"

I smiled, buoyed by my success. "Let's go and find out," I said.

Willow looked at her phone. "It's almost four o'clock," she said. "Let's wait until tomorrow morning, and in the meantime — how about I take your sign to the top of the footpath into town? You are supposed to be running a shop after all."

"I only got back two days ago," I laughed. "I'm *supposed* to be having some time off, but go on — put the sign out. Let's earn some money."

As Willow carried the A-frame sign up the short footpath into town, I tidied the shop area up a little and went outside with a cup of tea to sit at the picnic bench and wait for her.

Less than five minutes after she'd returned, the first customer appeared at the bottom of the footpath and made her way across the grass towards the boat.

"You put the sign the right way around them," I laughed.

"My name is not Susie Huggins!" Said Willow. "Of course I did."

When I'd first had the sign made, Susie had put it at the top of the footpath on the day I opened for business. Susie being Susie, though, she'd placed it on the wrong side of the path with the arrow pointing into town instead of towards the canal. Luckily, it didn't take too long for people to realise that a floating witchcraft shop on a narrowboat would more than likely be on the canal, rather than in the town centre. Mr Jarvis from the greengrocers had kindly turned the sign around for me when two people had come into his shop asking for directions to my boat.

"How quaint!" said the customer, looking at the *Water Witch*. "What a wonderful idea — a shop on a boat."

"Oh, there's plenty of them," I said. "There's even floating marketplaces on weekends in some towns along the canal. There's floating hairdressers, floating cafes, floating sweet shops. You name a type of shop, and there's probably a floating version."

"Well, this is just the sort of thing I've been looking for. I've always wanted to try my hand at witchcraft. Perhaps you could give me some advice on where to begin."

Willow and I led her into the small shop, and she gazed around at the shelves. "I don't know what I'm looking for," she admitted.

Ten minutes later, she left the shop with a smile on her face, a beginner's book on witchcraft, a small cauldron, a chalice, and an athame.

Willow helped me as more people found their way to the shop, and we made a good team, with Willow taking money and giving change, and me offering advice to customers.

As six o'clock approached, and the shops in town began closing, the trickle of customers slowed and I left Willow to count the takings as I made my way up the path to collect my sign.

With the sign under my arm, I'd got no further than a few feet back down the path, when I heard a softly spoken male voice from behind me. "Are you closing?"

I turned to look at him, and swallowed the smile on my face. Short sandy coloured hair, muscles, and tattoos. It was undoubtedly Granny's badboy, but he looked far from bad. His red eyes told the story of a man who'd been crying a lot, and Granny would have been disappointed at the state of his clothing. His t-shirt was crumpled and needed ironing, and his jeans had muddy marks on the knees.

"Y — yes," I stuttered, looking around for somebody to help me if he did turn out to be a crazed murderer. "I'm closing."

His face crumpled. "I was hoping you could help me. I read your sign, it says you can make potions to heal all ills."

I had to get that sign reprinted. The *heal all ills* line had come back to bite me in the backside on more than one occasion, and it seemed like this time it had attracted a suspect in a murder case. Maybe *potions for a wide range of troubles,* would be more advisable. Anyway, I certainly didn't have a potion that relieved people from the guilt of murder.

I glanced around again, but the street was quiet. No one was going to help me, and my magic was certainly not at the standard needed to prevent a thug attacking me.

"I'm sorry," I said, desperately searching for a lie. "I need to get back to my boat... I've got to get ready for my self-defence course. It starts in half an hour — I'm trying out for my black belt tonight."

He rubbed his eyes with his fingers. "Maybe a bottle of whisky would be a better potion," he said, looking at me one last time and turning away.

I ran the full length of the path, ignoring Mabel who yapped at my heels as I sprinted across the grass, and threw the sign on the ground. "Willow!" I shouted, as I leapt aboard the boat, almost losing my footing as I slipped on the decking. "Phone Barney!"

BARNEY ARRIVED QUICKLY, and after listening to my story and radioing the information in to the police station, he came aboard the boat. "Are you okay?" he said, putting a hand on my shoulder.

"Yes, I'm fine. He didn't do anything, it was just a bit of a shock seeing him and wondering if he was the man who'd killed Sam. I've never met a murderer. As far as I know, anyway."

"We don't know that he is. But it does seem odd that he was waiting outside the lawyer's office for Sam," said Barney, "and several people have alluded to the fact that Sam had a gambling problem. Maybe he was being forced to sell his properties to pay off his debts. Sometimes you've just got to put two and two together, but it would make my job far easier if that uptight lawyer would just tell me what he knows."

Barney cursed as he banged his head on a ceiling light. "Sit down, Barney," I said. "Narrowboats aren't made with people like you in mind."

He sat down next to me on the sofa, rubbing his head as Willow brought me a glass of wine. She sat opposite us, on my wicker chair, and leaned forward. "Will they find him?" she said.

"Every available police officer is out looking for him. It's harder in a small town like this without cameras everywhere, but hopefully they'll find him soon. I don't want you staying here tonight alone though, Penny," said Barney. "It's too secluded. Can you go to your mother's? Either that, or I'll stay here with you. They don't need me for the search, apparently."

"Willow's offered to stay with me," I said.

"Even though Mum's making lasagne tonight," sighed Willow. "That's sisterly love right there. Mum's lasagne is the best, especially when she's got the ingredients from the hav — "

My warning scowl stopped her before she said something that might have given our secret away. It was a silly mistake to make, but she quickly recovered. "From the half decent deli in Covenhill."

I changed the subject quickly. "Are you offering every boat owner on the canal in Wickford your company for the night, Barney?" I teased.

I knew he was going to blush even before he did, but it still made me smile. "No," he said. "Just you."

"I think it's very kind of you, Barney," said Willow, "and I think it's a good idea. Even though we don't know if he did kill Sam – you did say the guy was well built, Penny, and you said he was going to get drunk on whisky. What if he decides he wants a potion after all and comes banging on the door at two in the morning? We couldn't fight him off if he decided to turn nasty."

I doubted Barney could either, but I kept my mouth tightly fastened. "Okay," I said. "It's very kind of you, Barney, but if you think the ceiling's low, wait till you find out how short the dinette bed is. I have a feeling your feet will be getting cold tonight."

Willow and Barney went ashore and threw sticks for Mabel as I prepared a simple meal of chicken wrapped in bacon, and a fresh salad. We ate it on one of the picnic benches and watched as a line of three colourful narrowboats passed by on the canal, their bow waves washing into my cutaway and gently rocking the *Water Witch*.

"They're probably on their way to the car show," said Willow. "Susie said there's over fifty visitor's boats moored up alongside the field, and hundreds of car owners camping there."

Boat owners moved around the canals continuously, most of them using a continuous cruising licence, which allowed them to moor up in one spot for up to fourteen days at a time before having to move on again. When a gathering like the car show occurred next to the canal, boat owners would come from all over to enjoy the community spirit, helping each other out with odd jobs that needed doing and enjoying the liberated lifestyle that only liveaboards understood.

"Are the police asking questions at the show?" I said, passing Barney some buttered bread.

Barney put together a chicken and tomato sandwich, and took a small bite. "Of course," he said, chewing. "It could have been someone Sam knew who killed him, or it could have been a complete stranger who wandered into town, got drunk, and picked a fight with him for no reason. We're questioning everybody who was camping out there when Sam was murdered, but that's a lot of people. It will take time, and without a witness we're practically blind."

I dropped a piece of cucumber for Mabel, but she sniffed disappointedly at it and looked at me with pleading eyes. I relented, and handed her a piece of bacon fat which she swallowed happily. I threw another piece onto the stern deck of the boat where Rosie was watching us suspiciously. She gobbled it up and jumped onto the roof, licking her lips, and curling up next to a potted plant.

"Our best bet is the man we're looking for," said Barney. "Maybe he's new in town and nobody knows him, or maybe he's from the car show. Somebody will recognise him from his description."

We finished our meals in relative silence, watching the sunset, and listening to the jackdaws chattering in the distance as they prepared to roost. As darkness fell, the three of us stepped aboard the boat carrying our empty plates. Mabel curled up under the picnic bench after thoroughly searching the area for dropped titbits, and Rosie followed us into the middle section of the boat, slumping onto her favourite seat and falling asleep.

I made sure all three doors were securely locked and made Barney's bed up for him. "If you hear anything during the night, wake me up," he said, as Willow and I made our way to my bedroom.

It did feel safer having Barney aboard, and within fifteen minutes of getting into bed, Willow was snoring softly, and I was close behind her.

CHAPTER ELEVEN

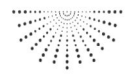

*B*arney left early in the morning after receiving a phone call telling him that a witness had come forward – a boat owner who'd seen someone walking along the towpath on the night Sam was murdered. He'd told the police that it had been too dark to see much, and he'd been drinking, but Barney rushed off to interview him in the hope he could jog his memory.

I'd prepared him a quick breakfast of boiled eggs and toast, and when I'd handed him a whole piece of toast, he'd quickly cut it into soldiers and proceeded to dip them in the runny yolks, licking his fingers clean when he was finished.

When he'd gone, Willow and I got ready for a visit to the lawyers. As Granny had said — leave no stone unturned, and I had a hunch that the information the lawyer was withholding could be important to the case. I dressed in a simple white t-shirt and shorts, and Willow borrowed a short flower print summer dress from me, which did far more for her figure than it ever had for mine.

"Do you need to look at the spell book again?" said Willow, opening the book at the persuasion spell.

I shook my head. "No, it's like Granny said. I know the spell is imprinted on my mind, and I just have to think about it. It's a strange feeling — not like the simple spells we're used to casting."

Willow slammed the book shut, and I sucked a little air into my mouth, tasting copper. I accessed the spell in my mind, and Willow looked at me with wide eyes as I clicked my fingers and she began moonwalking towards the bathroom singing *Thriller*.

"What are you doing?" I joked. "I thought you didn't like Michael Jackson?"

She hit a high note and span on the spot, scaring Rosie, before moonwalking back towards me. I let my mind go blank and Willow fell laughing onto the dinette seat. "Okay!" she said. "You've got the hang of it, but my wrath will be swift and fearsome when I learn that spell myself — I'll make you do the YMCA dance in the middle of town!"

We continued laughing as we locked up the boat and headed up the footpath into town. It would only take a few minutes to walk to the town centre, and we both needed some exercise. We admired the vintage cars we saw passing through town, although with most of them already at the show, there were only a few on the roads.

Police cars patrolled the area, no doubt looking for the mystery man, and Willow stopped to look at a poster in a shop window asking for information concerning the murder of Sam Hedgewick.

"It's a terrible thing, isn't it?" said a voice from behind us.

"Hello, Veronica," I said, her voice and the scent of her rose water perfume giving away her identity before I'd even turned to face her.

She pointed at the poster. "It's awful. Sam's father is beside himself, the nurses in the home have had to sedate him three times."

"Poor man," said Willow. "A parent should never have to bury their child."

"There's a terrible doom and gloom in the home," said Veronica. "I've popped out for a while to get some sun, and to pick some herbal medicine up for Ron." She held up a paper bag to show us.

"Is he okay?" I said.

"He just needs a little pick-me-up," she explained. "That potion you made him didn't help with Snoopy, but it certainly helped him sleep. He needed the rest, mind you — he was always in that gym. He's hurt his hand too, he strained it lifting a weight that was too heavy for him."

"Even Olympic athletes need a break now and again," said Willow. "It will do him good."

"I think he's having withdrawal symptoms from the exercise," said Veronica. "He's very agitated. I hope he doesn't have that thing that body builders suffer from. Now, what was it called again?" She tilted her head as she considered. "Road rage, that's it."

"Roid rage," I smiled. "You're not telling me Ron was taking steroids, are you? I'd have never made him a potion if I'd known that."

"Oh gosh, no! Ron always says his body's a temple. He wouldn't sully it with nasty drugs."

Willow put her hand on Veronica's. "It's not roid rage then, Veronica. He'll be fine."

Veronica nodded. "I know," she said. "It's just a very stressful time at the home. Everybody's concerned about Sam's father, and I overheard a nurse suggesting the murderer might strike again! The nursing home would be a very easy target for him to find his next victim in. Especially on a Wednesday night."

"A Wednesday?" asked Willow, furrowing her brow.

"Spotted dick night," explained Veronica. "The chefs make it for pudding every Wednesday after dinner. It's very rich, and most folk go to bed early after eating it, especially Sylvia. She thinks people don't see her, but she always sneaks a second helping." Veronica's face whitened. "The killer could easily sneak in and knock one of us off!"

"I very much doubt it's a serial killer," I reassured her. "The police are looking for a suspect, and Barney's gone to interview a witness. It won't be long before they catch whoever did it."

Veronica looked at the floor. "And to think my last words to Sam were nasty ones. I'm ashamed."

"Why? What happened?" said Willow.

"He drank too much at the party," said Veronica. "And then he wanted to drive home! I told him in no uncertain terms that he would do no such thing! We parted ways on harsh words, and then he couldn't get a taxi so he had to walk home." Veronica shook her head. "To think he was killed on the way. Maybe I should have just minded my own business and let him drive. He'd still be with us."

"He could have killed an innocent person, or himself in a crash. You did the right thing, Veronica," I said, placing my hand on her shoulder. "Come, on. Willow and I will walk you home."

The nursing home was a grand old building set in acres of manicured gardens. Once a mansion that had housed a local wealthy landlord and his family, with an army of servants, it had been an easy job to transform it into an upmarket residential home.

As we neared the steps, guarded by stone lions on pillars, which led to the large doors, a voice came from our left. "This door's open."

A short overweight woman peeped through an open doorway surrounded by climbing ivy, and Veronica waved her away. "Sylvia, get back inside. Don't use that door during the day — you'll give the game away!"

Sylvia hurried back inside, muttering to herself, and closed the door behind her.

"Give the game away?" I said. "What game's that?"

Veronica looked around, making sure nobody could hear her. "People use that door to sneak their lovers in at night," she smiled, oblivious to our shock. "The alarm's broken, so the nurses don't know when it's been opened."

"Naughty, naughty," I teased.

"Not me of course," said Veronica. "But I might need that door in the future, me and Ron are going through a rocky patch, you see. He's such a jealous man, but you can't blame him — look at me, I still turn the heads of men under sixty!"

"I'm sure you'll work things out," I said, helping Veronica up the steps.

"I hope so," said Veronica, "but I won't be told

what men I can and can't talk to. My ex-husband tried that little trick on me, and we were divorced before he knew what had hit him! I'll give Ron a month or two to sort himself out, but you know what they say, a leopard never spots a change."

"A leopard never changes its spots," said Willow.

"Yes, that's it. Come on girls, now you're here you can come and say hello to him. He's sitting in his room moping, two pretty girls like you will soon cheer him up."

We followed Veronica into the home, saying hello to the receptionist that sat behind the huge dark wood desk, and waving at the residents who sat in the large communal lounge watching TV. Ron's room was at the end of a corridor lined with potted plants and oil paintings, and Veronica tapped lightly on the door before letting herself in.

"Visitors, Ronald!" she said.

Ron looked up from a seat in the corner. Veronica hadn't been exaggerating when she said he'd been in the gym a lot. His muscles bulged at the striped pyjamas he was wearing, and he'd added inches to his shoulders.

"Oh, hello girls," he said in a flat voice. "Veronica told me you were back in town, Penelope."

"Cheer up, Ron," said Veronica. "Penelope and Willow don't want you bringing them down. Turn that frown upside down and get dressed."

"I don't feel well," said Ron. "I'm not trying to be miserable."

"You're not being miserable," I assured him. "You look very tired though."

"I'll be okay soon enough," said Ron. "Another good night's sleep should see me right."

"Come on, Ron," urged Veronica, "get up out of that chair and take a shower. What is it you always say? The devil's hands are lazy."

"The devil makes work for idle hands," muttered Ron.

Veronica nodded. "Yes, that's it. You wouldn't have lounged around all day when you were in the army, would you? They'd have kicked you out of that seat soon enough!"

"I'm not in the army anymore," said Ron. "I can sit here for as long as I like."

Veronica tutted. "Look at his pictures, girls," she said, pointing to the framed photographs that were perched on a set of wall shelves. "You wouldn't think it was the same man, would you?"

The fact that most of the photographs were black and white told me that Ron probably didn't feel like the same man these days. A lot of years had passed since Ron had posed for the photographs, some of them of him standing with other soldiers, and some of them portraits of him alone on top of a tank.

I ran my finger along the printed names of the

soldiers below a group photograph until I found Ron's name. "A sergeant. You did well, Ron." I said.

"I did okay," said Ron.

"Cup of tea, girls?" said Veronica. "I'm going to make one for Ron with extra sugar. Let's see if we can't get his energy up a little."

"No thanks," said Willow, placing a photograph back on the shelf. "We have to be somewhere."

"Well, be sure to pop in whenever you feel like it. Don't let Mr Grumpy put you off visiting us, he'll be right as rain in no time."

We promised to visit again, and made our way back into town, pausing outside the lawyer's office before we went in. "Do you think we need an appointment?" said Willow.

"Let's find out," I said, pushing the door open and striding inside.

The waiting area was sparse, with three plastic seats for clients, a fake rubber plant in a corner, and a middle-aged woman sitting at the tiny reception desk in the corner. Her face lit up when she saw us. "Are you here to see Mr. Sandler? He'll see you right away."

We didn't need an appointment, it seemed. I doubted that Mr. Sandler was inundated with clients in a town as small as Wickford, but he must have been doing something right to afford the BMW that gleamed in the sun, alongside the office.

"Thank you," I nodded. "We'd love to see him."

She hurried from behind her desk and knocked on the panelled wood door to the right of her work space. She pushed it open and led us in. "Two clients to see you, Mr. Sandler," she said.

The lawyer spun his seat around to face us, smiling at us over the vast expanse of wooden desk. "Thank you, Louise," he said.

Louise left the room and Mr. Sandler indicated the two seats reserved for clients. "Please sit down, ladies," he said, his tongue tracing his top lip, and his eyes on Willow's chest for far longer than was polite. I'd feel absolutely no guilt about casting a spell on a man who openly ogled my sister in that way.

Willow seemed unfazed. She even leaned across the desk to shake the lawyer's hand, bending far too low for my thin summer dress to keep her assets captive. Maybe I wouldn't need a persuasion spell after all. Mr. Sandler held onto Willow's hand for a few seconds too long, and smiled at us in turn as we sat down. He crossed his legs, picked up a pen which he rolled between his fingers, and flashed a bright white set of teeth at us.

"How can I help you, ladies?" he drawled.

Willow looked at me and smiled. "Why don't you ask him, Penelope?"

I returned her smile, and accessed the persuasion spell, sucking in a small amount of air and immediately tasting copper. It seemed I was a faster learner than Granny had given me credit for. I clicked my fingers beneath the desk.

"Mr. Sandler," I said, my head gently throbbing.

"Derek, please," he replied.

He didn't look like a Derek. More like a Brad, or a Pierre. Looks could be deceiving though.

"Derek," I smiled, already imagining what I wanted him to do. I took my phone out, brought Barney's number up, and slid it across the desk. "That's PC Dobkin's phone number. The police man who came in to ask you why Sam Hedgewick had been to see you on the day he was murdered. I'd like you to ring it from your phone and tell him what he wanted to know."

Derek picked up his phone from the desk and gave me a wry smile. "I'm afraid I can't do that," He said with a wink. "Client confidentiality, you see."

He turned my phone around and glanced at the number as he keyed it into his own phone. Confusion crossed his face, and I smiled sweetly at him as his eyes narrowed. "I really can't do that," he said, bringing the phone to his ear. "I could lose my licence."

He stared at me and Willow in turn. "I'm sorry," he said, "the police will just have to wait until they get their warrant."

"Ah, hello, PC Dobkins," he said. Barney must

have answered. "I've reconsidered. I will tell you why Mr. Hedgewick came to see me." His eyes opened wide as he spoke, and his hand trembled as he attempted to move the phone from his ear.

I concentrated hard, and Derek visibly shuddered.

"I asked Sam to come and see me," he continued, his face becoming whiter by the second. "His soon to be ex-wife had been in to see me the day before. She seemed quite desperate. She wanted to know all about the properties Sam was selling. She said Sam was leaving her for someone else and intended to move abroad. She seemed quite panicked about what would happen to her financially. I felt it was my duty to inform Sam."

He listened as Barney spoke. "No," he said, "I wasn't breaking client confidentiality in that instance. Mrs. Hedgewick was not a client, you see." He nodded as Barney spoke. "I'm sure you will get straight on it, PC Dobkins," he said. "Good luck with your investigation."

He put the phone down slowly and stared at me. He rubbed his head with his hands and pressed the intercom button on his desk. "Please cancel the rest of my appointments for the day," he said when Louise answered. "I don't feel myself. I need to go home and have a lie down."

"You have no more appointments today, Mr. Sandler," said Louise.

"That makes your job easier then, doesn't it?" he snapped. He pointed to the door. "You two should leave," he said. "I don't know what just happened, but I don't feel right."

With the spell still fizzing in my mind, I stared at Derek. "I suggest you don't tell PC Dobkins that we were here. You decided to phone him out of a sense of moral obligation, not because I asked you to."

He stared at me open mouthed and nodded.

"Thanks for your help, Derek," said Willow, offering him her hand again, which he refused with a quick shake of his head. "I hope you feel better soon."

CHAPTER TWELVE

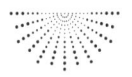

"I think it was a drunk stranger, on the towpath, with the windlass," said Susie.

I didn't put my theory forward that it was Sam's wife. We hadn't told Susie and Granny about our trip to the lawyer's office yet. Mum didn't know we'd blackmailed Granny for her spell book, and she'd have never believed that Granny would simply have handed it over to us. She'd have found out about Granny's accident with Boris and Charleston within minutes.

"I bet it was my badboy. I bet Sam owed him a gambling debt and he called it in, using the only method an alpha male like him knows... violence, intimidation, and ultimately, sad as it may be — murder," said Granny, spooning a second helping of lasagne onto her plate. "This isn't half bad for reheated food, Maggie," she said.

"It was far tastier last night," said Mum, choosing to keep her suspicions as to the identity of the murderer to herself. "Willow would have known that if she'd spent the night here, where she lives, instead of staying on Penelope's floating emporium of loneliness, in fear for her life."

Willow scowled. "There's nothing lonely about Penny's boat," she said, wincing as she snapped a piece of garlic bread off the steaming hot baguette in the centre of the table. "And no one was in fear for their life."

"Thanks to Barney," said Mum. "I'd have been far less happy about you two staying there last night with a potential murderer casing the joint, if that strapping young man hadn't been there to look after you both." Mum looked at the wall clock. "He's beginning to go down in my estimation though. I invited him for a family evening dinner as a thank you for saving my daughter's lives, and he decides he's going to be late."

"He'll be here soon, Mum," I said. "He's involved in a murder investigation, remember? And that's a *little* more important than lasagne and roasted vegetables."

"And he didn't save our lives," said Willow, stabbing a piece of courgette with her fork.

"I read your story in the newspaper, Susie," said

Mum, refusing to acknowledge Willow. "It was very informative and very well written."

"Thank you, Maggie," beamed Susie. "The police have asked me not to write about their ongoing investigations, so I'll have to wait until they catch the murderer before I write a follow up piece."

Mum nodded as Susie spoke, her hands clasped beneath her chin. "Well, I'm sure it will be just as gripping as the one I read today, dear."

"I'm going to the car show tomorrow," said Susie. "The classical car magazine still wants a story, it's Saturday tomorrow, and I could do with a day out. Maybe I'll have a wine or two while I'm there."

Mum smiled her approval, before standing up. "I think Barney's here," she said, as the sound of a car engine floated through the open window. "I'll let him in."

As soon as Mum had left the room, Granny looked at Susie. "I'm assuming these two tattle-tales have told you about my accident with Boris?"

Susie looked at me, and I nodded my permission. "Yes," she said. "It wasn't your fault though."

Granny waved her hand in the air. "Who's to blame is a ship long sailed," she said. "Speaking of ships, you girls are going to do me a favour. And if you refuse, you'll see exactly what blackmail is — and I don't mean that amateur stuff you pulled on me yesterday — I'll take you to hell and back! You mark my words!"

"Okay, Granny," I said, leaning back in my seat to put as much space between us as possible. "Calm down. What do you want?"

"Two birds with one stone," she said, speaking quickly as Barney's car door slammed shut and Mum shouted hello to him. "Boris heard about the car show on the radio, and wants to visit it. He's also a big fan of boats. I want you to take him to the car show on your boat. The show finishes on Sunday morning, so tomorrow's his last chance."

"We can't," I protested. "He's a goat, Granny. Goats don't admire old cars."

"Or go for boat trips," offered Willow.

Granny smiled. "Of course he can go on a boat, and on the radio it said there's a mixed livestock competition being held at the car show tomorrow. Enter him in that if you must. I'll even plait his beard. He'd like that."

"A livestock competition at a car show?" I interrupted.

"Yes," said Granny. "Along with a tent for bands to play in, with a bar. They've got rides for the kids too, and stalls selling all the usual tat. Boris will have a wonderful day out."

The front door slammed shut and two sets of footsteps echoed down the hallway. "I'm not doing that," I hissed. "It's ridiculous!"

Granny gave me the smile she reserved for people who were about to regret crossing her. "I will come down on you so hard you won't know if you're a witch or a warlock."

"I think it's a wonderful idea," said Susie, her face white. She'd seen Granny angry before and her expression told me she didn't want to see it again if she could avoid it. "I'll come on the boat with you, it'll be fun."

"What will be fun?" said Mum, breezing into the kitchen with Barney hot on her heels, ducking to avoid banging his head on the doorway.

"The girls have decided to take Penelope's boat out for the day tomorrow," smiled Granny, raising her eyebrows at me, her glasses sliding dangerously close to the tip of her nose. "They're going to the car show. I'm sure they'll have a wonderful time."

Mum rolled her eyes. "Each to their own," she said. She looked at Barney. "Do you see what all the fascination is with boats?"

"Leave Barney out of your campaign to get Penelope off that boat," snapped Granny. "He's an officer of the law."

Barney looked at his feet, but he couldn't hide the redness that rose in his cheeks. He really was too easy to embarrass.

"Scoot up, Willow," said Granny. "Let Barney have your seat, he and Penelope probably want to sit together."

It was my turn to blush, but Barney seemed happy with the idea, and sat down next to me as Willow made her seat available. I ignored Granny's cringingly overt matchmaking attempt, and poured my new neighbour a glass of iced lemon water.

Mum slid a plate heaped with food in front of him. "Tuck in," she said, "you'll need your energy if you're going to catch the killer."

Granny offered Barney some garlic bread. "Are you any closer to finding out who murdered that poor man?" she said.

Barney looked around the table. "I'm not really supposed to say anything," he said, picking up his cutlery. He glanced nervously at Susie. "Especially with a journalist in the room."

Susie swiped a finger over her chest in the shape of a cross. "You have my word, as a responsible freelance journalist, that anything you say will not make it into print."

"Or on the internet?" said Barney suspiciously.

"Or on the internet," confirmed Susie with a smile of encouragement. "Anything you say will stay at this table."

Barney took a bite of lasagne, made an exaggerated sound of appreciation, and nodded his approval at Mum, who shrugged. Everything she cooked tasted good, and annoyingly, she knew it.

"There's not much to tell, really," said Barney. "We're waiting for the test results on the windlass and the results of Sam's post-mortem. We're no closer to finding the man who was seen arguing with Sam, and the boat owner witness I interviewed this morning can only confirm it was a male he saw on the towpath near the Flirting Kingfisher."

"The Flirting Kingfisher?" said Willow.

Barney sipped his water and reloaded his fork with food. "Sorry, that's the name of his boat — *The Flirting Kingfisher*. He says the man was wearing a blazer or jacket with some sort of logo on it, but he can't recall what. It was dark, and he'd drank a few whiskies."

"It's something to go on at least," said Susie.

"That's not all that happened today," said Barney, puffing out his chest. "You know that lawyer I questioned?"

"Yes," I said, shifting in my seat and ignoring Willow's smile.

"My hard-line questioning paid off," said Barney. "He obviously realised I wasn't to be messed with, and today he crumbled — he couldn't take the heat I'd brought down on him. He phoned me and told me exactly what I needed to know. Sergeant Cooper's very impressed. He even gave me a coffee break."

"And what was it that the lawyer told you?" said Granny, giving me a proud look of approval.

Barney told everyone what Willow and I already knew, and then blew out a frustrated blast of air between his teeth. "That was a waste of time too," he said. "We'd already questioned her when Sam's body had been found, but she'd failed to mention they were getting a divorce, or that she'd been to see the lawyer."

Granny slammed her fist down on the table, making everybody jump. "Guilty!" she declared.

Barney shook his head. "No, she's got a watertight alibi. It transpires that Sam was leaving her for somebody else because she'd been cheating on him for years. She was with the other man on the night Sam was killed, and they've got witnesses. They went out for a meal in Covenhill, and the restaurant staff say they left at half eleven. The taxi driver told us he took them back to the man's house in Covenhill. Sam's wife spent the night there."

"That smells fishy," said Willow. "Why didn't she tell the police they were getting divorced when you first spoke to her?"

"Money and shame," said Granny, adjusting her glasses. "She wanted to make sure she kept up the pretence of being his loving wife to ensure she gets all his assets, and she was ashamed that she'd been to the lawyer on the very day he died — to try and keep her dirty cheating hands on his properties and cash."

"I couldn't have put it better myself," said Barney, making Granny swell with pride.

"What about the woman Sam was leaving his wife for?" said Mum. "Maybe she killed him."

"Sam's wife doesn't know who she was, and we can't find any evidence pointing to her," explained Barney. "We're working on the theory that she never even existed. We think it was a smoke screen so Sam could finally leave his wife. She refused to leave him because she'd lose out on his money, so maybe Sam was stuck in an unbearable situation and needed a way out."

"What about gambling?" I said. "Did you find out if he's in debt?"

"There's no evidence of it," said Barney. "But serial gamblers don't tend to leave paper trails. It's all hearsay at the moment, but we really want to speak to the man we're looking for. Maybe Sam owed him money."

"What a wicked web we weave," murmured Granny. "Anyway. Enough of this doom and gloom. Maggie, didn't you say you had a bread and butter pudding in the oven? I'm still peckish."

WITH THE BREAD and butter pudding demolished, and everyone beginning to get tired, I decided to cycle back to my boat and see to Rosie's needs. I refused the offer of a lift from Barney, and reassured everyone that I'd be all right on my own for the night.

Granny followed me out of the cottage as I was leaving and watched me getting my bike out of mum's car. "So, you made a spell work. You got that lawyer's tongue to wag."

"It wasn't so hard," I said. "Not as hard as you said it would be, anyway."

Granny shook her head. "Those spells *are* difficult, give yourself some credit. Some of them even I've never mastered. You did well. You're going to be a powerful witch someday, Penelope. It won't be long before Maeve gives you your entry spell if you carry on as you are. Just keep practicing, and remember that once a spell is imprinted in your mind, you'll never need to learn it again."

"Unless I get witch dementia," I smiled, freeing a pedal from the lip of the car boot.

"My spells are still up here," said Granny, tapping the side of her head with a finger. "They're just more muddled up than your relationship with Barney is."

"There is no relationship with Barney," I said, looking away. "Just a friendly one."

"You'd better tell him that," said Granny. "Didn't

you see the way that cute little freckly face of his lit up when he knew he could sit next to you?"

I sighed and swung my leg over the bike. "I'm going now, Granny."

"I'll bring Boris to your boat first thing in the morning, and don't you dare leave without him."

"You have my word," I said.

"Good. It will give me chance to drive into Covenhill without worrying about him. I need to buy one of those computer things."

I took my foot off the pedal and stared at her. "What in the name of the goddess do you need with a computer? You said the manufacturers rape the land for the rare elements they need to make them."

"It's not a crime to have a change of opinion," said Granny, pushing her glasses up her nose. "Anyway, it's not for me. It's for Boris."

"Two questions. Why are you paying for a computer for Boris, and why does a goat even need a computer?"

"I'm not paying for it," said Granny. "Boris is letting me take Charleston's credit card. He's a very wealthy man — the acupuncture was more of a hobby than a job. He didn't need the money if his bank balance is anything to go by. He wants to start one of those blog thingy's, I'm not really sure what they are, but Boris is very excited at the prospect."

"But he can't use a computer. He's got hooves!"

"Precisely what I said," agreed Granny. "Boris came up with a solution though — voice recognition software. He just needs to speak to the computer, it all sounds very clever."

"It all sounds like madness," I countered.

"You let me and Boris do what we like, young lady. Anyway, a new hobby will do him good. He's far too fond of the brandy, he needs something to keep him occupied."

"You said brandy couldn't harm his body, what's the problem?"

"He can still get drunk, and he gets a little ... problematic, when he's three sheets to the wind."

The conversation was becoming too surreal. "I'm going, Granny," I said. "As much as I'd like to stand here all evening talking about an alcoholic tech savvy goat, I want to be back at my boat before it gets dark."

Granny waved me off, reminding me with a scowl that I wasn't to leave without Boris in the morning. I pedalled quickly, and within fifteen minutes I was leaning my bike up against a picnic bench and patting Mabel on the head as she sniffed at my boots.

I stepped aboard the *Water Witch* and grabbed some incense from one of the shop shelves as I passed, lighting it on top of the wood burner, and giving Rosie a belly rub before feeding her and settling down at the dinette table with the spell book.

I chose a spell that sounded like it could be useful,

and silently read the symbols and letters until my head throbbed. Sucking a small amount of air into my mouth, I tasted copper and concentrated on making the wilting plant in a pot on the kitchen counter come back to life.

A searing pain made me gasp, and I slammed the book shut, making Rosie jump. Granny had been right – some spells were much harder than others.

When the pain in my head had subsided, I opened the book again and read a few random spells, my head throbbing, but not hurting, as the symbols imprinted themselves on me. Any spells that began making my head hurt I ignored, and went onto the next one. After twenty minutes of study I closed the book, placed it in the storage area beneath the dinette seat, and prepared myself for bed. Maybe I would get to visit the haven sooner than I'd imagined, I certainly felt more magical, and I was beginning to understand how exciting it must be to finally be granted the entry spell.

CHAPTER THIRTEEN

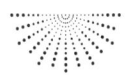

*G*ranny and Boris arrived at the boat ten minutes after Susie and Willow had arrived together. I knew better than to ask Granny how she'd managed to get Boris into her car — it would probably have been very intolerant of me to assume a man in goat's body couldn't mange the simple task of sitting in a car. Boris had a collar around his neck, and Granny held onto the end of a dog leash as she guided him across the clearing. Boris's beard was just as Granny had promised, and a small piece of red ribbon was tied around the tightly woven plait. The goat — or man. I still hadn't quite made my mind up — looked happy enough to be led by Granny, but I still confronted her about the new development in her treatment of Boris.

"What are you doing?" I said. "Surely Boris doesn't like being led around like your pet?"

Boris spoke for them both as Granny removed the backpack she was carrying and placed it on one of the picnic benches. "It was my idea, Penelope," he said. "To avoid arousing suspicion from any quarter today, I suggested the dog leash. If you're going to be taking me to a public place it seems sensible to treat me like this. You might receive unwanted attention otherwise. I mean, it's not many goats that walk side by side with their owners around a field full of vintage cars, now, is it?"

He had a point. "Okay," I relented, "but you just let me know if that collar starts hurting you."

"That collar won't hurt!" spat Granny. "It was the most expensive one in the pet shop. It's a comfort fit."

"And very nice it is too," said Boris. "I think the red breaks up the white of my hair, and it matches the ribbon in my beard."

Granny placed an affectionate hand on the goat's head. "You're sure to win the competition, Boris. You look like a million dollars."

"Gladys has cleared a space on the mantelpiece for the trophy, just in case I win," said Boris. "The last trophy I won was for being in the winning crew in the boat race against Cambridge university. I love boats, and I can hardly wait to get aboard yours, Penelope."

"Come on then," said Susie, arriving at my side. "I'll show you aboard, Boris."

As Susie led Boris to the bow of the boat and helped him negotiate himself aboard, Granny passed me the little backpack. "There's a little bottle of brandy in there," she said. "Give him a sip before the competition – it will give him confidence. There's some chocolate biscuits in there too, and a brush for his hair. You make sure he wins that competition, Penelope. He may not show it, but he's got his heart set on coming first."

I took the bag and smiled as Granny looked over my shoulder, watching Boris as he disappeared down the steps into the shop. "You really like him, don't you?" I said.

Granny sighed. "It's lovely having an educated man, I mean goat, around the house. I hadn't realised how lonely I was until Boris moved in with me. You be sure to look after him today, Penelope. I'm holding you accountable for his safety."

"He'll be fine," I promised. "Now you go and buy his computer for him. I'll bring him back to you tonight."

Granny waved at Boris as he peered through one of the boat's windows. "Have fun, Boris!" she called.

"I will!" came the muffled reply.

Granny turned her back and hurried toward the

footpath to the hotel and car park. "Don't bring him back too late," she shouted. 'I'm cooking for him!"

When Granny had vanished into the trees, I stepped aboard the boat, lifted the engine hatch in the stern deck and checked the oil levels. Willow untied the mooring ropes and joined me next to the steering tiller as I prepared to start the engine.

Susie appeared at the bottom of the steps that led from my bedroom, with Boris behind her. "Don't you dare start her up without us," she said. "Boris really wants to watch."

With all four of us standing on the stern decking, it was crowded, but we had enough to room to move about. Boris watched as I turned the key in the ignition and pressed the engine start button.

"What a beautiful sound," he shouted over the noise as the old diesel engine burst into life, vibrating beneath our feet. "They don't make them like that anymore!"

He was right. The engine in my boat was from the nineteen sixties, and it chugged away at a far slower pace than modern diesel engines.

Willow had given the boat a small push as she'd jumped aboard, and we were already floating slowly away from the bank.

I pulled the control lever backwards, putting the gearbox in reverse, and the propeller churned the water behind us as I grabbed the long steering tiller and began reversing the boat onto the main body of the canal.

"Well done!" shouted Boris, as I manoeuvred the long boat. "You're quite the expert!"

As the bow cleared the turning to my mooring, I put the boat in neutral and straightened up as the boat continued to float backwards.

"Can I have a go of driving?" asked Susie, stroking Rosie, who sat on the roof in front of us.

"Of course," I promised, "just let me get us going."

Looking down the long roof, past the potted plants and the chimney, I aimed the bow of the boat and selected forward gear. The engine throbbed beneath us, and the boat began slowly gaining speed as water churned white behind us. With a speed limit of four miles an hour imposed on the canal system, we were never going to break any speed records, but we chugged along at a pleasant pace, and I stood aside to let Susie take the controls.

"Push the tiller in the opposite direction than you want to go," I explained, as Susie steered us towards an overhanging branch.

She straightened the boat up, and Boris gazed around happily at the fields that took the place of trees on the opposite bank. The bank on our side of the canal was lined with walls and cliffs which homes and shops sat on top of, with people in some of the gardens who waved cheerily at us as we passed.

Steam rose from the Wickford brewery chimney, and the smell of yeast in the air made Willow scrunch up her face in disgust. "That's why I don't drink beer," she said. "It's horrible."

"There's nothing like a real ale on a Sunday afternoon," countered Boris, sniffing the aroma. "It's an acquired taste, but when you acquire it, it will be with you for life."

Susie kept the boat in a straight line, and slowed down as we passed moored boats, preventing our bow wave from disturbing them. It would take an hour to get to the car show, and we had one lock to negotiate on the way. We passed under one of the bridges that attached one side of Wickford to the other, and Willow dragged her hand down the stone walls as we chugged beneath it, the engine echoing in the confined space. The canal beneath the bridges was barely wide enough for my boat, and any boats coming in the opposite direction would have had to give way and wait for us to pass under the bridge before continuing their journey.

"Would you mind if I went to the bow deck?" said Boris. "I can't drive with these hooves, so I'm just taking up space back here."

Willow laughed. "Come on, I'll go with you," she said, leading Boris down the steps into my bedroom.

They walked the length of the boat before emerging on the bow deck, sixty feet in front of us. I leaned out and looked down the side of the boat, smiling as Boris planted both hooves on the tip of the bow and held his head high in the air. "Are you having fun?" I yelled.

"I'm on top of the world!" he shouted, eliciting giggles from me and Susie.

Ducks and swans swam alongside us, and soon we approached the area of canal where Sam had met his untimely end.

A small cliff rose from the towpath on our left, and we passed beneath the Lock and Key pub, saying a few words for Sam as we spotted the police tape still wrapped around a tree trunk, the other end floating in the margins of the canal.

"The lock's just past the next bridge," I said to Susie, trying to take my thoughts off the murder. "Do you want to go ashore and operate it, or shall I ask Willow?"

"I'll do it!" said Susie.

We passed beneath the final bridge in Wickford, and the lock came into sight a hundred metres to our front. I slowed the boat as we approached it, and Susie grabbed the windlass she'd need to open the gates. The windlass was an L-shaped metal tool that was used as a winding lever to operate the heavy lock gates, and I winced as I imagined how it had felt for Sam, if he had indeed been murdered with one.

As the boat neared the bank, Susie prepared to leap ashore, and when the gap was only a few inches she made the jump and hurried to the first set of gates. Boris and Willow joined me on the stern deck as I steered the boat towards the entrance to the lock, and stood either side of me as I moved the boat forward. The lock was set in our favour, with the first set of gates open and the second set holding back the water in the canal above us.

The walls of the lock loomed fifteen feet above us on either side of the boat, with barely three inches between the hull and the stonework. Soon, Susie would close the gates behind us and open the gates in front of us, flooding the lock with water and turning the high walls into the low banks of the canal.

When the boat was safely clear of the gates behind us, Susie used the windlass to operate the gate mechanism, trapping us between the two sets of thick nineteenth century wooden gates. She waved as she climbed the grassy hill and shouted down to us. "Ready?" she asked.

"Go on," I shouted, "open them!"

As the gates to our front opened, the boat floated upwards like a cork in a glass being filled with water. I kept the engine engaged in forward gear, applying just enough power to prevent the wash of incoming water pushing us backwards, and soon we were floating fifteen feet above the stretch of the canal behind us, with the rest of the canal stretching ahead of us.

I pulled the boat ashore a few metres past the gates, and waited for Susie to get back aboard, a big smile on her face and the windlass safely in her hand. With everyone aboard, I pulled away from the bank and we continued our journey, admiring the beautiful countryside that had opened up on both banks.

CHAPTER FOURTEEN

*B*oris gasped as we rounded the bend in the canal and the festival fields opened up on our left. "Wow," he said. "That's quite a sight."

It was quite a sight, and quite a smell. Chrome shone and twinkled for hundreds of metres as the sun bounced off the rows and rows of cars, and the scent of frying onions and bacon wafted through the air from the assorted vans and stalls selling hot food of all kinds.

More delicious cooking aromas drifted from the line of colourful boats that were moored up alongside the canal bank, and the sound of children's laughter, and music coming from the big tent in the middle of the field lifted my spirits. I was going to enjoy myself, I realised with a smile.

In the field adjacent to the one the cars were on

show in, lines of tents, caravans, and camper vans dotted the landscape.

It was the last day and night of the show, and people seemed to be making the most of it. Groups of men and women sat in huddles on the grass near the canal, drinking beer and wine from plastic cups or cans, and other people wandered along the rows of vintage cars, admiring the old machinery.

It was a real festival atmosphere, and we began to make plans as we cruised past the lines of boats, searching for a mooring spot for the *Water Witch*.

"How about we look at some of those magnificent cars," suggested Boris, the ribbon in his beard fluttering in the gentle breeze, "then get a hotdog and a beer. It's been too many years since I savoured food bought from the back of a greasy van."

"That's a great idea, Boris" said Willow, "I'm starving!"

All the best mooring spots had been taken, but finally we found one, at the end of the long line of boats, beneath an old gnarled oak tree surrounded by bushes. I manoeuvred the boat into the space and Willow jumped ashore to tie the *Water Witch* up. With the engine switched off, the sounds of the show were even more vibrant, and I picked Rosie up from off the roof and ushered her inside the boat. "You stay in there," I said. "It's far too busy and loud for you out here."

She gave me a look that I interpreted as a thank you, and sauntered off to relax on her favourite seat.

"Let's go," said Susie, hooking her camera bag over her shoulder and stepping onto the grassy bank. "My camera finger's itching to get some photos of those cars."

Boris leapt gracefully ashore and waited as I attached the dog leash to his collar. "Don't worry, Penelope," he said quietly as I apologised. "I really don't mind, and I couldn't ask for a nicer person to be on the other end of my leash."

I was beginning to realise why Granny had such a soft spot for him. He really was a charming goat.

"Come on," I said, "let's go and have a nice day."

We walked alongside the line of boats, saying hello to the boat owners that sat on their roofs, drinking and eating, and telling us what a lovely looking goat Boris was. Boris made low sounds of appreciation at every compliment he received, and even allowed a friendly old lady to tickle him behind his horns.

We were just about to veer off to the right, and away from the canal, when Willow grabbed my arm. "Look," she said, pointing at a beautiful yellow and purple narrowboat. "It's the *Flirting Kingfisher*. The boat that Barney's witness lives on."

The boat had a fresh paint of coat and the windows gleamed like they had been very recently cleaned. A man wearing just shorts sat on a deckchair on the bow of his boat, sipping a drink and reading a book. His chest and shoulders were bright red, and I guessed he'd be applying an aftersun soothing cream by the end of the day.

"Do you feel like trying some magic?" said Willow with a suggestive grin. "To see if we can get more information out of him than Barney could?"

Without warning, a spell popped into my mind, almost begging me to cast it. "A spell of enhanced memory," I said. "It's just made itself known to me. It must have imprinted on me last night when I was flicking through Granny's book."

"Do it," urged Susie, "you might make him remember something that solves the murder."

Boris agreed. "I'm not privy to the story about this witness, but I'd love to see some magic in action."

"He saw someone on the towpath," I explained to Boris. "He said there was a logo or something on his jacket, but he can't remember what."

"Then help him remember," said Boris in a low voice, being careful not to let anyone hear him speaking. "There's still a murderer at large."

The man looked up from his book. With three girls and a goat staring at him, I felt it was necessary to explain our interest in him.

"I'm sorry to bother you," I said, approaching the boat. "I'm a friend of the policeman who interviewed you about the man you saw on the towpath on the night Mr Hedgewick was killed."

He looked at me with confusion on his face. "How on earth do you know it's me?" he asked.

"The boat name," explained Willow. "We're on a boat too, my sister lives on the canal, like you. We just want the murderer caught. It scares me to think of my sister alone on her boat at night with a killer on the loose. A killer who's already killed someone on the canal towpath."

His guard visibly dropped when he knew I was a liveaboard. Boat owners always helped each other whenever they could, and Willow's fear-mongering seemed to have made him even more willing to talk to us. "It is unnerving," said the man. "But I told the police everything I remember."

"Can I ask you a question or two?" I said.

"Of course, but as I've said. I can't remember much. It was dark and I was drunk." He winked at me. "Whiskey's my weakness," he added with a smile. He gestured at us with a wave of his hand. "Come aboard," he offered. "Would anybody like a drink? I'm getting myself a top up."

We refused the offer of a beverage as we stepped aboard the *Flirting Kingfisher* and sat together on one of the hulls curved built in benches. The boat owner stepped down into his boat, and Boris remained on the bank with his leash tied off on the bow of the boat. "I would have liked one of what he was drinking," he complained. "I was surprised to find out what good noses goats have, and this excellent nose tells me that the golden liquid in that gentleman's glass is not a whisky bought from the supermarket."

"You can have a brandy when we finish speaking to him," I whispered, tapping the backpack Granny had given me.

The boat owner emerged from the belly of his boat with a full glass, and reclaimed his seat. He took a sip of whisky and looked at us in turn. "Okay," he said. "How can I help you?"

"I want you to try and remember what you saw that night on the towpath," I said. "What was the man you saw wearing? What was the logo you said you saw on his jacket?"

He looked up and to the right as he thought. "Like I told your policeman friend," he said after a moment. "I can't remember. He was quite far away, and he was only lit up by the moon for a second or two."

I accessed the spell and tasted copper. "Try again," I urged, my head gently throbbing. I clicked my fingers behind my back. "What was the logo or badge on the man's jacket?"

He sucked his bottom lip into his mouth. "I'm sorry," he said. "I really can't — "

He paused, and excitement flashed in his eyes. I

concentrated harder. "Do you remember something?" I said.

"Wow," he murmured. "I do." He looked at the drink in his hand. "It must be this stuff," he marvelled. "It's as if I can zoom in on my memory. It's all becoming clearer!"

I took a deep breath. "What did you see?"

He scrunched his eyes up as he concentrated. "He was wearing a blazer or jacket," he said softly, his eyes still screwed tightly closed.

"What did he look like?" I whispered, as Willow and Susie both leaned forward, watching the man.

"I can't remember his features," he said. "I can just see the badge on his clothing, but it's not clear."

I sucked more air through my teeth, and the taste of copper filled my mouth and throat. "What was the badge on his blazer?" I said slowly.

He straightened in his seat. "Wait," he said. "I can see something. A crown and letters. There was a crown on the badge with letters below it!"

My head pulsed as I concentrated. "What were the letters?" I said.

He took a long breath. "The letter B," he said. He shook his head. "No, it was an R. Then an A, and the last letter was a C!" He opened his eyes. "RAC!"

"Can you see anything else?" I urged.

"No," he said, with a perplexed expression on his face, "but my head hurts. It must be this whisky. It' a special blend I got from a distillery in Scotland. It's very strong."

Boris leaned over the hull wall and put his mouth next to my ear. "Told you," he murmured.

Susie tapped me on my leg. "Look," she said, pointing at one of the old cars near to the canal bank. "Look at the badge on the front."

The old car's polished paintwork shone in the sun, and heat waves rose from the warm metal. The badge Susie was pointing at was attached to the grill at the front of the car, and I smiled as I studied it. RAC was written in large letters with a crown above them. I stopped the spell, and the man's face went blank. "It's gone!" he said. "I can't picture it anymore."

"I think you've given us everything we need," said Susie.

"RAC," said the man. "That's the Royal Automobile Club. Most of the owners of these cars will be members of the RAC," he said. "It's a huge club. Do you think the murderer is here? At the car show?"

"I don't know," I said. "But I need to let the police know what you told us."

He drained the last of his whisky and massaged his forehead. "Be sure to tell your police friend that I gave you the information. I was very disappointed that I couldn't help him when he came to my boat asking questions."

"I will," I promised. I took my phone from my pocket. 'I'll tell him right now."

Barney didn't answer his phone, so I sent him a text message instead, telling him where I was and what I knew. "I've told him the information came from you," I said to the man as I climbed off the *Flirting Kingfisher* and joined Boris on the bank. "He'll be very happy."

Susie and Willow followed me off the boat, and we left the man looking pleased with himself as he headed back into his boat to top his glass up again.

"What do we do now?" said Susie, snapping a photograph of a man dressed in old fashioned clothes changing a wheel on his car. He pumped the jack handle up and down, and cursed as it slipped and hit his finger.

Even I recognised the car as an old Rolls Royce, and joined Boris in admiring it. "There's not much we can do," I said. "If the murderer did come from the car show, he could be long gone, or he could be anybody here." I looked around the huge field and estimated there to be well over two hundred cars. "Lets just enjoy our day, and if we see anything suspicious, we can let the police know. It's up to them now. They're still looking for Granny's bad boy, so we can keep an eye out for him too, but right now I'm hungry. Who fancies a burger?"

CHAPTER FIFTEEN

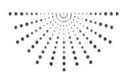

*W*e chose a burger van with a relatively short queue of people waiting to be served. Two children fussed and patted Boris as we waited. He did his best to act like a goat in a petting zoo; nuzzling the children's hands and accepting the blades of grass they fed him, spitting them out in disgust when the children's parents had been served and the family had left with their meals.

"I will do most things expected of a goat," said Boris under his breath, ejecting the last of the grass from his mouth. "But I won't do that."

It was our turn to be served, and I left Boris standing next to Willow as I approached the food van. The white van was emblazoned with large red letters which read *Mr. Meaty*. The vendor was far from meaty though, and I doubted he ate any of the greasy products he sold. I ordered our food and passed it around as it was served. A hotdog with onions for Susie, a cheeseburger for Willow, and a chicken burger for me. Boris chose a triple burger with bacon and cheese with a side of fries, and I scowled as I refused Mr Meaty's offer of a spork.

We found a secluded area away from the crowds, where Boris could speak freely, and sat beneath the shade of a horse chestnut tree, watching people go by and enjoying the scent of the wild flowers that flourished in the the hedgerow behind us.

Boris ate his meal with less decorum than I would have expected from such a cultured individual, but I supposed eating without cutlery or fingers *could* only finish in a mess of sauces and food scraps. No sooner had he licked the last of the mustard from the cardboard tray, he looked up at us. "I'd like a dram of brandy now please, young ladies. I need a boost of confidence for the show."

We'd checked what time the mixed livestock competition was starting, and had watched as people had begun arriving at the makeshift circle of hay bales, some leading pigs and sheep, and a few with goats, which Boris had eyed with envious suspicion. There was still half an hour to go until the show started, so I opened Granny's backpack and took out the bottle of brandy and the saucer she'd provided.

Willow and Susie styled Boris's hair with the brush Granny had provided as he slurped brandy from the saucer. When he'd had six saucerfuls, I wiped the remains of his meal from the hair around his mouth, and tightened the plait in his beard.

"How do I look?" he said, wobbling slightly as he walked back and forth in front of us. "I'd better look good. I'll blame you three if I don't win the competition. You see if I don't! I'll tell Gladys that you messed up my chances by feeding me that fast food rubbish!"

"You look drunk, Boris," said Susie, taking a photograph of him.

"And you sound drunk," said Willow. "That wasn't a very nice thing to say to us."

Boris looked at Willow and gave what I assumed he thought was a smile. In reality it was a grimace which showed off his yellowed grass worn teeth. "You know I love you, don't you? I love all of you. I bloody love — "

"That's enough, Boris," I snapped. "I'll put a spell on you if you don't stop swearing and start behaving. I'm sure I've seen a sleeping spell in Granny's book."

Boris tilted his head from side to side and mimicked me in a high-pitched voice. "*I'm sure I've seen a sleeping spell in Granny's book*!" he teased. He stamped his hoof. "Get over yourself, Penelope

Pitstop. You couldn't *spell* spell! Let alone cast one on me!"

Willow burst into laughter, and Susie continued snapping photographs of the drunk goat.

"Granny said he gets problematic when he's had a few brandies," I whispered to Willow and Susie. "I didn't think she meant she meant this problematic though."

"What are you saying about Granny?" demanded Boris, lowering his head and waving his horns at me. "I'll ram you if you say one bad word about her. Just try me. Go on, I dare you. Say one bad thing about that wonderful woman and see what I do! Go on, I dare you. I double dare — "

"Right, that's it!" said Willow. "Now you're just being rude!" she scrunched her face up and clicked her fingers. Boris's shouting stopped immediately, but his mouth continued opening and closing as he tried to speak.

"Where did you learn that?" I said, impressed.

"You're not the only one who learnt a few spells from Granny's book," she said with a wink. "A spell of silence. I learnt it for the next time mum teased me about my..." she looked down at her chest, " ...boobs."

"Look at him," laughed Susie. "He's writing something in the dirt."

Boris dragged his hoof through the dry dirt at the base of the tree we sat beneath, and Willow stood up to read his message. "Give me my voice back," she read. "You can't silence me, you bunch of — " Willow wagged her finger at the goat. "No, Boris! that's rude! I won't read that, and you can't have your voice back yet, that spell lasts for three hours."

Boris rammed the tree in frustration, the thwack of horn on wood gaining the attention of a young couple walking past. Willow grabbed him by the horns. "Calm down, Boris," she demanded. "Or we won't enter you in the show. I'll put you in that field behind us with the cows, and pick you up when we're ready to go if you can't behave."

Boris struggled to release his horns from Willow's grasp, stamping his hooves into the ground.

"Right, I'm phoning Granny," I said, retrieving my phone from my pocket. "She'll sort him out."

Boris looked at me with alarm and stopped struggling, he scratched his hoof through the dirt again. "I'll be good," read Willow. "Don't phone Gladys. It's not me talking. It's the brandy. It's a weakness."

I slipped my phone back into my pocket and looked at Boris with my sternest of stares. "You're going to behave?" I asked.

He nodded and stumbled as Willow released his horns, almost falling over completely.

"Are you sober enough to enter the contest?" I said.

Boris nodded again, opening his mouth as he tried

to speak. He nodded once more and I smiled at him. "We've all had too much to drink at one time or another, Boris. Maybe you should stay off the brandy though? It doesn't seem to agree with you."

Boris dropped his head in shame and staggered over to Susie, dropping to his knees beside her. He nudged her camera with his nose, and Susie laughed. "You want to see the pictures I took of you?"

Boris nodded, so Susie turned her camera on and showed him the large screen on the rear. He shook his head shamefully as Susie flicked through the pictures of him hurling abuse at us.

"Don't worry," said Susie. "I'll delete them."

Willow glanced across the crowd of people to our front. "It looks like Boris's competition is starting soon. We'd better get over there and sign him up before it's too late," she said.

Susie held onto Boris's leash as we made our way through the cars and people, pausing now and again to admire any particularly beautiful vehicles. When we got to the circle of hay bales surrounded by onlookers, and full of people with their animals on ropes next to them, Susie went to the judges table to sign Boris up for the competition, and Willow and I took a seat on a scratchy bale of hay.

"Who's going to lead him round the ring for the judges?" said Willow.

I took a coin from my pocket. "Heads or tails?"

"Tails as always," said Willow. "If it's tails, I win, and you parade him around the ring."

I flicked the coin and caught it in one hand, slapping it onto the rear of the other. "Heads it is. Make sure he behaves."

CHAPTER SIXTEEN

Willow led Boris into the ring and stood between a woman with a very grumpy looking pig, and a man with a particularly woolly sheep — far too woolly for the warm weather in my opinion. The sheep looked happy enough though, and tried to sniff Boris's face, who reacted by turning his nose in the air and looking the other way.

Willow gave us a nervous smile as a man's voice burst out over the tannoy system. "Ladies and gentlemen! It's the show you've all been waiting for — the Wickford and Covenhill beautiful farmyard animal of the year competition!"

I glanced around at the crowd. There were no more than twenty spectators, and most of them looked like they were only there to use the hay bales as make shift seats to enjoy their beer on.

The man continued. "This year, I'm proud to announce the return of the 2014 winner — Harry the pygmy goat! Give him a big round of applause!"

A mild smattering of clapping caused a nervous Shetland pony to buck his rear legs, and the owner, an equally nervous looking woman, calmed it with a hand on its head.

The tannoy crackled again. "Without further ado, let's get the show on the road! The rules are simple. The animals are to be walked around the ring three times, and after the last lap, each animal is to be halted in front of the judge's table so they can admire them and make their final decision! Competitors... begin your walk!"

A competition official, who stood in the middle of the circle of animals and owners, waved her arm and directed the competitors in a clockwise direction around the ring. Some animals tried to resist their owners, particularly the pig who led the way in front of Willow and Boris. He grunted and pulled at the leash around his neck, causing his owner to almost drag him along behind her. Boris displayed no such reluctance to show off. He lifted his head high, and still a little unsteady on his feet, began to trot. Ripples of applause spurred him on, and Willow glanced at us nervously as the goat bounced over the sun dried earth beside her.

"Unbelievable!" came the excited voice over the

tannoy. "A goat doing dressage! Will you look at that ladies and gentlemen — that's the best trained goat I've ever seen!"

Boris lifted his legs higher with each stride he took, and danced along next to Willow, his snout pointing at the blue sky and his chest puffed out before him.

The owner of Harry the tiny pygmy goat, stared at Boris in disbelief, and tugged firmly on her animal's leash. The little goat didn't take favourably to her bullying tactics, and dug his hooves into the dirt, dropping his head in protest and refusing to move.

Boris continued showboating beside Willow, and as they passed the dissident pygmy goat, he sneaked a sly hoof beneath the little goat's rear leg and tripped him up. Harry sprawled on the floor bow legged and gave a little bleat of shock, which Boris ignored.

A man behind me laughed and broke into loud applause. "That goat's amazing!" he shouted.

Susie turned to look at him. "His name's Boris," she smiled. "And yes, he is rather amazing."

He clapped even louder. "Go, Boris!" he yelled. "You've got this!"

Willow and Boris had drawn the stunned attention of the other competitors, who stared in disbelief as Boris trotted around the ring, occasionally glancing at the three judges behind the trestle table and offering them hideously toothy smiles.

The nervous Shetland pony dragged its owner towards a spectator eating a hotdog, and an angry looking ram butted the pig in front of it. The official in the ring pointed at the space in the hay bales that acted as an entrance. "That ram is disqualified!" she shouted. "No aggressive animals allowed!"

"But that weird goat tripped the pygmy goat!" the owner protested. "Why is he still in the competition?"

"I didn't see any such incident," said the official, watching Boris as he drew more attention from the crowd. "Get that ram out of my ring!"

The ram's owner begrudgingly led his animal out of the ring, and Boris celebrated by wriggling his rear end at him.

The man behind me shouted again. "Go, Boris!"

Other spectators joined his supportive shouts, whistling, yelling and clapping. The sound of the crowd's excitement attracted more people to the ring, and as the crowd swelled in size, so did Boris's ego. Some of the other animal owners had given up trying to win, and stood still next to their animals as Boris raised himself onto his rear legs and stepped in time with Willow. He looked to the left and right and smiled at the people who cheered him on.

"Boris! Boris! Boris!" chanted the crowd.

Even the judges joined in, banging their fists on the wooden table in time with the chants of Boris's newfound groupies.

"This is going to make an amazing story," said Susie, snapping photographs of Boris and Willow. "He really knows how to work a crowd!"

"The brandy may have turned him into an angry drunk," I said, "but it's certainly given him confidence!"

The official in the ring waved her arm. "The third lap is complete. Bring your animals to the judges table one at a time!" she yelled over the noise of the ever growing crowd.

Willow and Boris joined the line of competitors as they took their turns standing in front of the judges. Boris gave gentle nods of his head to the spectators as they continued to shout their support for him. People erupted into louder cheers as Boris lowered himself to the knees of his front legs and took a low bow.

"I think it's safe to say he's won," said Susie as the judges called Willow forward, all three of them standing up and clapping as Boris stood before them.

Boris raised himself onto his rear legs, and I put my hand over my eyes, watching him through my fingers. Boris was taking it too far. "What's he doing?" I said.

The tannoy crackled. "I'm lost for words!" the excited man shouted. "A pirouetting goat!"

Boris span furiously on the spot, his front legs tight against his sides and his nose pointing high above him. Willow had dropped the leash, and it span in the air around Boris as he gained momentum.

"Look at him go..." murmured the man behind me, "...beautiful."

It was quite beautiful. The plait in Boris's beard whizzed through the air, and dust swirled at his feet as he span faster and faster. A blurry white whirling dervish, Boris transfixed the crowd as he wowed the judges and drew envious looks from the other animal owners.

"We have a winner!" shouted one of the judges — an elderly female with snow white permed hair. "Ladies and gentlemen, I give you the winner of the Wickford and Covenhill beautiful farmyard animal competition — Boris the dancing goat!"

The crowd cheered, and a lady beside me held her phone up as she filmed the show. "This is going on the internet," she said excitedly. "It'll go viral!"

Boris slowed his spinning and lowered himself onto all four legs. He wobbled a little as he tried to regain his balance, and fell in a heap at Willow's feet. He sprawled on his back with his legs straightened out above him like a dying fly, and his chest heaved as he panted.

"Get that goat some water!" shouted the official.

"He'd prefer brandy," said Susie, with a giggle.

A man ran into the ring with a bucket of water and splashed some on Boris's face. Willow helped Boris onto his front, and he slurped greedily at the water, occasionally lifting his head to nod his thanks at the chattering crowd.

"When he's recovered, bring him forward for his rosette and trophy!" shouted a male judge. "He truly deserves them, and so do you, young lady," she said to Willow. "That is the most well trained animal I have ever seen."

My phone vibrated in my pocket. I took it out and looked at the screen. It was Barney.

Susie was already on her way to join Willow and Boris in the ring, her camera ready to catch the prize giving action, so I backed through the crowd to a quieter area and answered Barney's call.

"Did you get my text?" I asked as I answered.

"Yes, and it ties in with new information we've acquired. We know who the mystery man is," said Barney. "We've got his name, his photo, everything. He's bad news, Penelope. I shouldn't be telling you this, but I wanted to warn you incase he comes near your boat again. He's our prime suspect now."

"Tell me what you know, Barney," I said, clutching the phone tight to my ear.

Barney continued, speaking urgently. "His name's Jason Danvers. We got in touch with all the tattoo parlours within a fifty mile radius, and one of them remembers him from our description. He did the phoenix tattoo on his arm." Barney paused for a moment. "Jason owns a casino, but get this — Sam owed him a lot of money, and Jason has got a police record for violence in the past. He's also got a warrant out for his arrest — he beat up somebody else who owed him cash and put him in hospital. I think it's safe to say that he's our guy."

"So where is he? Are you any closer to finding him?"

"We've got a photograph of him. It won't take long, but if you see him again, please stay away from him and phone me straight away. He's a dangerous man. I don't like the thought of you at the car show. We've found out he has a small collection of classic cars, and that matches neatly with the information the witness gave you about the badge on his blazer. We're checking with the Royal Automobile Club to see if he's a member." He paused momentarily. "How did you get that information, Penny? That witness was adamant he couldn't remember anything."

"He was drinking whisky again," I said, thinking quickly. "He thinks it jogged his memory."

"That makes sense," said Barney. "There's more too. The results have come back from the suspected murder weapon and Sam's post-mortem."

"And?" I urged.

"The coroner found a lot of alcohol in his stomach, and what he thinks are drugs. He's sent a sample off to the toxicology department to be analysed."

"Sam Hedgewick on drugs?" I said. "Really?"

"If he was mixing with violent gambling men, who knows what else he was into," said Barney. "Anyway, the windlass wasn't the murder weapon, but the wound on Sam's head was definitely made with a cylindrical metal object. There's small imprints on Sam's skull — the pathologist says they could have been made by some sort of hand grip on the weapon. We're thinking the handle of a car jack, based on the information my witness gave you, and the fact that Jason is involved with cars. It's an assumption, but the best one we have."

I remembered the man I'd watched changing the Rolls Royce wheel. A jack handle certainly had the potential to be used as a murder weapon.

Barney continued. "I'd prefer it if you took your boat back to the hotel," he said. "Just until we've caught him, and make sure you're not alone tonight. We've put road blocks around Covenhill and Wickford, so if he is still in the area, he might try and walk out following the canal towpath."

Cheering erupted from the circle of hay bales, and Willow, Susie, and Boris walked past a line of clapping people towards the entrance. Boris had a red rosette pinned to his collar, and Willow was carrying a small silver trophy.

"We're about ready to leave," I assured Barney. "We'll head back to the boat right away."

"Good. I've got to go, Penny," he said. "We're on our way to the car show. When we get there no-one will be able to leave until we've searched the place from top to bottom. So unless you want to stay there, I suggest you leave now."

I said goodbye to Barney and shouted to the others to join me. They made their way towards me with several people still following Boris, taking photographs and videos and patting him on his head and back. "Are you sure you won't let me interview you, Willow?' shouted a man with an open notebook. "It would make a great story!"

"No thanks," said Willow. "How I trained him is my secret, and it's staying that way."

"Plus, I'm writing the story," laughed Susie as she neared me. "There's going to be so many videos of Boris on the internet, somebody needs to lie about how he was trained to pirouette."

The distant sound of police sirens reminded me we had to hurry. I quickly explained everything that Barney had told me, and we rushed to the boat, climbing aboard and starting the engine as the police sirens grew louder and the first of the cars sped through the gate on the opposite side of the field in a cloud of dust.

Other boat owners stood on their roofs to see what was going on as I guided the *Water Witch* past them, and soon we were out of sight of the car show and heading towards the lock.

"My head hurts," complained Boris, "from alcohol, and from shame about the way I spoke to you lovely young ladies. I'm truly sorry, and highly ashamed of myself."

"Don't feel bad, Boris," I said, steering the boat around a gentle bend in the canal. "You've been through a lot recently. Anybody in your position would want to let their hair down a little."

Willow agreed. "Don't let what you said to us ruin the memories of your competition performance. You were outstanding, Boris."

"You were," nodded Susie. "I doubt any animal is ever going to beat that performance."

I laid my hand on the goat's back. "Why don't you have a lie down?" I said. "Go on, use my bed."

He looked up at me with thankful eyes. "I think I will," he said. "Thank you, Penelope. The offer of a bed to sleep in is one of the kindest gestures a person can make."

Boris climbed down the two steps from the deck into my bedroom, and jumped up onto the bed. He walked in three circles and plopped himself down, falling asleep almost immediately.

Willow followed him into the boat, placed his trophy next to him and draped a blanket over his back. Rosie mewled, and leapt up alongside him, sniffing him and curling up next to his chin, joining him in sleep.

WITH THE LOCK BEHIND US, and a crowd of ducks following the *Water Witch,* we negotiated the last of the bridges between us and my mooring, and Willow took over the steering duties for the last ten minutes of the journey. She expertly guided the boat closer to the bank on our side of the canal as another narrowboat approached from the opposite direction. We shouted hello to the frizzy haired man who drove the other boat as we glided past one another, and he gave us a friendly wave.

I left Willow in charge of the driving and stepped down into my bedroom to wake Boris. Susie had offered to drive him home, and I wanted him to look respectable for Granny. Not hungover and tired.

I shook the goat gently, and Rosie sniffed at my hand. "Boris," I said. "We're nearly home. Would you like a bowl of black coffee to help with the hangover?"

He opened his eyes and yawned. "That would be wonderful, Penelope," he said. "And one or two of those biscuits that Granny packed for me would compliment the coffee perfectly."

I helped him down off the bed, and Rosie leapt to

the floor with him. "I'm going to take a stroll through the boat and onto the bow deck," Boris said. "The breeze on my face will make me feel better."

"Good idea," I said. "Can you manage the doors to the deck on your own?"

"I've learnt a lot of things since being in this body," said Boris, "and opening doors was amongst the first. This mouth is very versatile, you'd be surprised."

I followed Boris as far as the kitchen, and began making coffee as he continued along the boat and brushed past the purple curtain into the shop area.

Watching a moving vista through the windows from inside my own boat was not something I experienced often, and I leant on my kitchen counter as the kettle boiled, watching the steam from the brewery chimney rising above the elm trees.

Something nudged my leg, and I looked down to see Boris staring up at me, his eyes wide with shock. "Don't say anything," he implored in a panicked whisper. "Your safety is at risk if you utter a single word. Join the others on the back of the boat, and get your phone ready. You need to speak to the police."

CHAPTER SEVENTEEN

I stepped up onto the stern decking with Boris close behind me and Rosie in my arms, who I placed on the floor at my feet. The sound of the engine was loud enough to disguise any conversation, but I still warned Susie and Willow to keep quiet. "Something's wrong," I said, the breeze ruffling my hair. I turned to the goat. "What is it, Boris?"

"I want you to all remain calm," he said in a low voice. "I opened the bow doors and stepped outside for a moment or two, but the smell from the brewery made me rather queasy. When I went back inside the shop, I thought I'd have a look around." Boris craned his neck and looked down into the boat. "Penelope, there's a man crouching behind the counter in your shop. I'm no detective, but from the description you've given us, I think it's safe to say he's the murder suspect."

Willow gasped. "But he's seen you, Boris, and he knows you've seen him. He'll kill us! We need to jump overboard and escape!"

"Calm down, Willow!" demanded Boris. "I'm a goat, remember. He looked a little shocked to see me, but I kept my cool and sniffed around his feet. I even licked his hand and nibbled some of those herbs in the box behind the counter. Very tasty they were too. He shooed me away and pushed himself further into the corner. We'll be fine if we carry on as we are."

I'd already dialled Barney's number, and he answered quickly. "Barney," I said, panic bulging in my throat. "The man you're looking for is on my boat. He doesn't know that we know he's onboard, but he's hiding in my shop. Jason Danvers is in my shop!"

Barney sounded more nervous than I felt. "Where are you?" he snapped, his voice cracking.

"A few minutes from my mooring," I said. "What do we do?"

"Carry on as if nothing's wrong," instructed Barney. "Moor up when you get back to the hotel, and get off the boat. We'll be there as quickly as we can. There's no police in Wickford at the moment, we're all here at the car show. It'll take us a while to get to you."

"Hurry, Barney," I said.

"I will, I promise." He paused for second or two. "Please don't do anything stupid, Penny. I'd hate for anything to happen to you."

"I won't," I said. "We'll get as far away from the boat as possible as soon as we moor up."

"Penny?" shouted Barney. "Are you there? I'm losing — "

I put my phone in my pocket. "He's lost his signal," I said. "But they're on their way. We've just got to carry on as if nothing's wrong. As long as we stay at the back of the boat until we've moored up, we should be okay, I doubt he'll do anything if he doesn't know we're aware he's onboard."

Willow closed and locked the stern doors. "That's a little safer," she said.

I pushed the boat's power lever forward and the engine throbbed, the propeller spewing water behind us. I had bigger things to worry about than a canal speed limit, and I gave the engine more revs than I'd ever given it before.

We stood together nervously, and Willow placed her hand next to mine on the steering tiller. "I'm scared," she admitted.

"It'll be over soon," I said. "Look, the entrance to my mooring is just around the next bend."

We kept quiet as I negotiated the final stretch of canal, and Boris kept his nose pressed against the pane of glass in the doors, looking out for movement inside the boat.

I slowed the boat as we approached the gap in the trees, and steered the bow slowly into the entrance, putting the gearbox in reverse to slow our momentum as we made contact with the bank. I turned the engine off and whispered to the others. "Get off the boat," I said. 'You tie the stern rope, Willow, and I'll do the bow."

The four of us climbed off the boat, Boris making a graceful leap ashore that even under the dangerous circumstances impressed me. Rosie decided the roof was a better option for her, and leapt onto it, licking her paw and watching us curiously.

Willow tied off the stern rope, and I walked to the front of the boat as casually as I could, incase Jason was watching me through a window. I had considered leaving the bow rope untied, but narrowboats had a habit of breaking away from their moorings if both ropes weren't securing them to the bank. Even though my boat couldn't have floated onto the main body of the canal, it would have made the police's job harder when they finally arrived.

A loud yapping sound echoed around the clearing, and Boris looked up in shock as Mabel sprinted over the grass towards him. "What on earth?" he said, backing away from the blur of white that approached him.

"It's okay," said Willow, 'it's only Mabel."

"Gladys told me about her," said Boris, "but seeing her in real life is vastly different than how I imagined."

Mabel ran at Boris, but Boris lowered his head and threatened her with his horns. "I've got no time for your nonsense, goose dog," he shouted. "We need to make good our escape!"

Mabel backed down as Boris charged her, and ran towards the front of the boat in panic, whining, yapping, and flapping her wings.

"No, Mabel!" I shouted, as the scared bird leapt onto the bow deck and scurried into the shop through the doors that Boris had left open.

"Get off me!" came a man's voice. "Get off!"

The boat rocked a little, and Mabel's vicious growls increased in volume.

"Get off me or I'll hurt you!"

"What do we do?" said Susie. "We can't rescue Mabel, the man in the boat is a murderer!"

Boris stamped his hooves. "Nobody's harming a fellow magical animal on my watch!" he yelled. Grass and mud flew from beneath his hooves as he sped towards the front of the boat. He leapt onto the bow deck, slipping as he attempted to take the tight turn through the open doors, and threw himself down the steps.

"Unhand that goose, you cad!" he shouted as he

disappeared from view, the clacking of his hooves on wood echoing through the clearing.

"We have to help!" I shouted, sprinting alongside the boat and clambering aboard.

The man shouted again, this time with fear apparent in his voice. "Help! What are you? What are you? No! Please don't bite me there!"

He screamed, and the pain in his voice made me wince. I jumped down the steps into the boat with Willow and Susie close behind me, and took stock of what was happening.

Jason's feet kicked and scraped along the floor as Boris dragged him from behind the small plywood counter, his teeth buried deep in the murder suspect's crotch, and Mabel sitting on his back, flapping her wings and growling. Downy feathers fluttered in the air around the goose, and she jabbed her beak in Jason's direction as Boris pulled him from his hiding place.

Stock fell from my shelves as the man struggled, and his screams of pain hurt my ears in the confined space.

"Boris! Leave him!" I shouted. I was sure I'd read that a man could die from a severe injury in the area that Boris was attacking. "You'll kill him!"

Boris relented a little, visibly relaxing his grip on the man's jeans.

"Will you stay where you are until the police get here if the goat let's go?" I said.

Willow grabbed an athame from a shelf and pointed it at the man. "I'll stab you if you try anything," she threatened.

The ritual witchcraft knife glinted in the dim light from the shelf covered windows and the doorway behind me, and Jason nodded frantically. "Yes!" he squealed, his voice far too high for such a muscle bound badboy. "Call him off!"

"Let him go, Boris," I ordered, "let's see what he's got to say for himself, starting with why he's on my boat."

Boris released the man and took a half step backwards. "I've got my eye on you," he warned. "If you make any funny moves I'll bite you so hard you'll be able to shatter glass with your voice."

"The goat's talking," the man said in horror. "The goat's talking to me."

"Nonsense," I said, winking at Boris, who acknowledged the message with a nod of his head. "You're hallucinating because of the pain you're in. Goat's can't talk, but you can, and you're going to answer some questions." The man nodded again, his thick tattooed arms between his thighs, his hands clutching his manhood. I continued. "What are you doing on my boat, and why did you murder Sam Hedgewick?"

He groaned as he held his crotch. "I'm on your boat because I heard the police arriving at the show. I've been living in a tent at the car show since the police started looking for me. Look at the state of me — I haven't had a change of clothes in days."

He certainly looked disheveled, and it explained why he'd looked so run down when I'd encountered him at the top of the footpath. His jeans were muddy, and his crumpled t-shirt hung limply from his large frame.

"Why my boat?" I said. "And how did you break in? The doors were locked."

He scrambled a few inches away from Boris. "It was the only boat that was hidden. It was at the end of the row and nobody could see me getting onto it. You should remember to lock the shutters on the side of the boat as well as the doors."

The last time I'd opened the shutters was during the barbecue. I made a mental note to check they were locked every time I left the boat.

Sirens wailed in the distance, and Boris snorted. Mabel flapped her wings and growled, and Jason squeezed his thighs together protectively.

"The goat talks and the goose is a dog," Jason mumbled. "What's going on here?"

"I'm asking the questions," I said. "Why did you kill Sam? The police know you did it. You'd better get used to small spaces like this, you'll be spending a long time in one."

Jason made a strangled sound in his throat. "I didn't kill Sam," he sobbed. "I wouldn't have harmed a hair on his head."

"You killed him because he owed you money," said Susie. "A gambling debt. We know all about you. One of our friends is a policeman, and he told us you've got a violent history and a warrant out for your arrest."

"I've done things I'm ashamed of," said Jason. "But I would never have hurt Sam. He helped me change who I was. We were moving abroad together so we could both have a new start. I loved Sam, I loved him so much."

He broke down into loud body shaking sobs, and I used a gentler voice as I spoke. "So you're the woman he was leaving his wife for, although obviously you're not a woman."

The police sirens got louder and then stopped. They'd arrived. It would take them less than a minute to run to my boat.

"She'd been cheating on him for years," Jason said, tears streaming down his cheeks. "When Sam couldn't pay his debt to me, I took pity on him and we became close. Sam wanted to sell everything he owned so we could buy a vineyard in Spain." His sobs got louder. "We were going to make wine! Sam loved Tempranillo!"

"Why did you stay in the area when you knew the police were after you?" I asked. "You could have been miles away by now."

He fixed me with an angry stare. "I wanted to stay around until the police found out who killed Sam. Whoever did it will wish they'd never been born when I get my hands on them."

I considered getting Granny's spell book and quickly learning a truthfulness spell, but it wasn't needed. I was convinced that Jason was telling the truth.

I looked at the door as a voice outside shouted my name. It was Barney. "Penny! Penny! Where are you?" he yelled.

"We're in here!" shouted Susie, poking her head through the doorway. "We're okay!"

Boris," I said, "take Mabel into my bedroom. I don't want her attacking anyone else."

Boris pushed through the purple room dividing curtain, and Mabel happily rode him, looking more content than she had for a long time. It seemed she'd found a new friend.

Heavy boots thudded on the boat's decking, and Barney appeared in the doorway with his nightstick in his hand. "You, stay still!" he shouted at Jason. Bone cracked on wood as he hit his head on the doorway, and he cursed as he came to my side. "Are you okay? Penny," he asked, grabbing me in a firm hug.

I waited until he'd released me, and gave him a reassuring smile. "I'm okay," I said. "We all are."

Sergeant Cooper stepped down into the shop and tripped on the bottom step. He hit the floor with a heavy thump and groaned.

"Are you hurt, sarge?" said Barney, going to his aid.

"I'm fine, Dobkins," he barked, getting to his knees. "Arrest that man!"

Barney handcuffed Jason, who was still crying, and read him his rights.

"I don't think he did it," I said.

Willow agreed. "I don't either."

Sergeant Cooper stood up. "And who do you two think you are, bloody Cagney and Lacey? Leave the police work to us, and you carry on selling this cheap tat." He kicked a wand and sent it skidding beneath a shelf unit.

Barney span on the spot, his face crimson with rage. "Don't you speak to them like that!" he yelled. "Say what you want to me, but if you ever speak to Penelope or her sister like that again, I'll lose my job because of what I'll do!"

I'd never seen Barney so angry, and pride swelled in my chest.

Sergeant Cooper opened his mouth to say something, but thought better of it. He turned away from us and began making his way up the steps. He paused and glanced over his shoulder. "I'm sorry," he said, looking at me and Willow. "That was highly unprofessional of me. It's been a busy day, and I've been under a lot of pressure trying to catch that man. PC Dobkins, make sure your friends are okay and then bring the suspect out."

Barney calmed down as quickly as he'd exploded. "I will, Sarge," he said, "and I'm sorry too. It's been a stressful day for us all."

Sergeant Cooper shook his head. "Sometimes people like me need reminding of a few things. I respect you for your honesty, Barney."

"He's never called me by my first name before," said Barney, as Sergeant Cooper stepped off the boat.

The handcuffs jangled as Jason got to his knees. "There was a talking goat," he said. "He bit me in the family jewels."

Barney clicked the button on his radio. "Can we get a drug testing kit ready for the prisoner, please?" he said.

"Affirmative," came the crackling reply of a woman.

Barney placed an arm under Jason's armpit and helped him to his feet. "Come on, let's get you down the station," he said. "You've got a lot to answer for."

"Barney," I said in a low voice. "I really don't think he did it."

"We'll find out soon enough, Penny," Barney said, guiding Jason to the steps. "He'll be questioned as soon as I get him back to the nick."

Susie, Willow, and I, followed Barney and Jason up the steps, and stood on the decking watching as the prisoner was escorted up the footpath with a policeman on either side of him.

"If he didn't do it," Susie said. "There's still a murderer on the loose."

"The police will find out soon enough," said Willow. "Who knows — maybe Jason's just a really good liar — there's still a chance he did it."

Boris's voice came from inside the boat. "Penelope," he said. "I'm looking at all the things that have been knocked off your shop shelves in the struggle, and there's a few items I'd like to buy for Gladys."

"Of course," I said, stepping down into the shop and joining Boris in the mess of stock that littered the floor. "Granny would appreciate a present. No charge though, Boris. Just take what you like."

"I'll hear no such thing!" protested Boris. "You don't run a business by giving things away. Of course, one of you will have to loan me some money until Gladys can go to a ATM machine for me."

When the shop had been tidied, and any broken stock reluctantly thrown in the bin, Susie fulfilled her promise of driving Boris back to Granny's and led him up the footpath to the car park.

He'd have quite a story to tell Granny when he got home, and in the backpack he'd put the gifts he'd chosen for her — a witch themed mug, a bumper sticker for her car, and a small metal tin that Boris said would be ideal for the mints Granny enjoyed sucking on.

Mabel watched on forlornly as her new friend left with Susie, and Rosie stood a few feet behind her, beginning to gain confidence now she'd seen that Boris trusted the goose.

Willow and I went inside and opened a bottle of wine. We deserved a drink, and Willow balanced her half full glass on her knee as she phoned Mum to explain what had happened, and to tell her she'd be staying on my boat again for the night.

"Mum wants us to have breakfast with her tomorrow," said Willow as she finished the call. She took a long sip of wine and gazed out of the window at the water and trees. "She also suggested I move onto your boat as I seem to be here more than at home." She took another sip of wine and smiled at me. "That's not such a bad idea, is it?"

CHAPTER EIGHTEEN

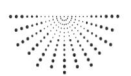

A pair of hands carrying a tray laden with croissants, muffins, and crumpets appeared through the shimmering sheet of blue that filled the doorway. The rest of Mum emerged through the light, and the spell fizzled out, returning the doorway to its intended function — an entrance to the lounge, and not a portal to a magical realm.

It was Mum's second trip to the haven in the space of ten minutes, and the kitchen table was laden with food prepared by Aunt Eva. "She's got the cooking bug again," explained Mum. "But this feast is to congratulate you for catching a murderer. She's very proud, she says bravery runs in our family."

"We didn't really catch him," I said. "He caught himself by stowing aboard my boat, and as we've already told you, we don't think he's guilty."

"That's not what it says in the newspaper," said Mum, laying the tray on the table. "Unless you're calling your friend a liar. It was Susie that wrote the article, and she was on the boat with you. I think she knows what happened."

"She's just reporting what the police are saying," Willow said, her hand hovering over a plate laden with crumpets. "She has to. It's her job."

"Where is she anyway?" said Mum, sitting down. "Eva made this breakfast for her too."

"The police are holding a full press conference," I said. "Barney's making sure she gets a front row seat."

"I hope the police commend you all on your courage," said Mum. "Although the whole incident yesterday has just made me all the more nervous about you living on that boat, Penelope. I mean, if a murderer can just sneak aboard, then you're hardly safe, are you?"

"I'd rather forget about the whole thing for now, and eat," said Willow, saving me from another of Mum's lectures, although I had to agree with her about my safety. It had been quite unnerving to find out how simple it had been for someone to break into my home and business.

"Eat what you can," said Mum. "I'll put the rest in Tupperware boxes and take some to your grandmother now I've got my car back. I need an excuse to go and visit her. She's still ignoring my phone calls, and I caught her watching me through her binoculars this morning. Nosy old thing that she is."

"You caught her watching you through her binoculars, how exactly?" said Willow, buttering a hot crumpet. She reached for the pot of plum jam. "While you were spying on her through your telescope by any chance?"

"It's my job to keep an eye on her!" snapped Mum. "She's elderly, and she has witch dementia. It's a daughter's duty to look after her mother. Especially in times of illness." She pressed two slices of freshly baked buttered bread together, sandwiching three slices of crispy bacon between them. "She has no need to be watching me, though! She should respect my privacy."

I waved my hand over the muffin on my plate. "There's a spell on this muffin," I said, impressed with how much progress I'd made with my magic over the previous few days. "But it's only one to help it rise in the oven. It's safe for me to eat."

Mum's eyes showed she was equally impressed. "Since when have you been able to do that, Penelope?" she said, staring at me. "The magic in that blueberry muffin is ancient haven magic. It should be well beyond your capability to detect it."

"Let's just say that Willow and I have been practising like you wanted us to," I said. "The days of you and Aunt Eva magically conspiring to stop me living on my boat are over."

Mum feigned shock, but not very well. "I'm glad that you've both been practicing," she said, "it makes my heart happy to hear that, but I'm hurt that you think I've been conspiring against you, Penelope. Those other spells were Eva's doing, not mine. To imagine that you think that poorly of me. Oh my!"

I bit into my muffin. "Okay, Mum. It wasn't you. I get it. I'll never mention it again."

Mum nodded. "Good. That's the ticket! Anyway, if anyone's conspiring, it's that grandmother of yours. I saw her driving that goat somewhere yesterday morning. She even put it in the front seat with a seat belt on!"

"Safety first," I said.

"Boris is a goat, Penelope! Goats shouldn't want to get into a car! Then I saw her coming home a couple of hours later without him, but she had shopping bags from that computer shop in Covenhill." Mum licked some bacon grease from her top lip and continued. "You tell me why she needs a computer! She specifically told me that computers were a way for the government to control us. That's why I've never bought one, and I really wanted one too."

"What do you want a computer for, Mum?" said Willow.

"One of the ladies at the Wickford rose and geranium fancier's club mentioned she can get all the music she wants on hers," Mum said. "When your dad left me, he took all my Lionel Richie records with him." Mum gazed upwards, with a twinkle in her eye. "I was so in love with that man at one time. He was my everything."

"Don't waste your emotions on that waste of skin," I spat. "Dad cheated on you and spent all your money. He spent no time with me and Willow, and he never looked for a job! You should be happy he left with that woman, Mum!"

"Not him, silly!" said Mum. "Good riddance to him! That's why you two carry my maiden name along with me. I want no memory of him at all. No, I was in love with Lionel Richie. Those eyes, that voice. The way he caressed his microphone. Of course, he's far too old for me now, but when I was a teenager he was my older man fantasy. I miss listening to him. That's why I wanted a computer."

I placed my hand on Mum's. "Get one then, I'll help you find all the music you want."

"Maybe in the future" she said. She slid her hand away from mine and picked up a crumpet. "Come on, let's finish breakfast, then the three of us are going to visit my mother. I want to know what she's up to."

I glanced at Willow, who shrugged her reply. She was right, we couldn't help Granny keep her secret forever, Mum was eventually going to find out what she'd done to Boris, however hard we tried to keep it from her.

I excused myself from the table and went upstairs, pulling my phone from my pocket. I could at least give Granny a heads up that Mum was calling to see her.

Granny didn't answer after thirty seconds, so I went into Mum's pristinely tidy bedroom. The colourful quilt she'd taken almost a year to make by hand was laid neatly on her bed, and photographs of family members decorated the large oak chest of drawers, with old pictures of me and Willow taking prime position at the front. I stood by the large window and gazed out over the woods and Wickford beyond them. The canal twinkled in the distance, and I could just make out the roof of the Poacher's Pocket hotel. Mum's huge telescope was pointing directly at Granny's cottage which was perched on the peak of the hill on the opposite side of the valley, and I closed my left eye as I looked through the viewfinder with my right.

I made sense of what I was seeing through the telescope, and grabbed my phone from my pocket. I rang Granny again, silently urging her to answer. Granny continued what she was doing in the garden, oblivious to her land line ringing inside her cottage. I tried once more and gave up with a sigh.

Oh well, I'd done my best. It would be up to Granny to explain to Mum why she was sharing cocktails in her garden, with a goat, at ten o'clock in the morning.

CHAPTER NINETEEN

*G*ranny obviously hadn't heard the car pulling up outside her home. Music floated over the roof of her cottage, and I winced when I heard the laughing voice of Boris.

"What in the name of all that is moral!" gasped Mum, slamming her car door shut and shoving the three Tupperware boxes at my chest. "Is she entertaining a man in her garden?"

Mum didn't wait for an answer from either me or Willow. She stomped alongside Granny's cottage, following the path past the lean-to which hid another of Granny's secrets, heading determinedly towards the back garden. Her hips swayed and her hair bounced, and Willow and I followed in her wake, casting nervous glances at each other, both resolved to the fact there was nothing we could do to keep Granny's secret any longer.

Mum rounded the corner of the cottage a few metres ahead of us, and her shriek made Willow jump.

I turned the corner just in time to see Mum holding a hand to her chest and staggering backwards, finding support from the trunk of a young peach tree which groaned under her weight. "What on earth?" she gasped. "What in the name of the goddess is going on?" She clutched my arm tight as I dropped the boxes and helped her stand up straight. "Tell me I haven't gone mad, Penelope," she mumbled. "Tell me that Boris is smoking a cigar and drinking what looks like a mojito. Tell me I'm not hallucinating."

Mum hadn't gone mad, and neither Granny or Boris had spotted us, or heard Mum's shriek. They continued what they were doing, oblivious to their audience. Granny was sitting in a deck chair at the bottom of the garden with a white sun hat on, clutching a glass in her lap. At her feet was a large glass jug, the mint leaves spilling from the top giving away the nature of the cocktail it contained.

Mum's gaze of horror was firmly fixed on Boris though. He lay on a tartan picnic rug with a glass beside him, from which protruded one of the curly straws Granny had bought for me and Willow when we were younger. To the front of him was my grandfather's vice which he'd used to tie his fishing flies. In place of a fishing lure, though, was a large cigar, on which Boris took a long drag and blew a cloud of smoke into the air, creating three perfect rings which Granny broke apart with a finger.

Granny laughed, her voice barely audible over the music which pumped from the radio beside her seat. The chickens in the nearby coop stared on in fascination, with one of the more intelligent ones using the diversion to peck at the pieces of corn that Granny scattered each morning. I hoped it was the chicken who'd squeezed out an ostrich egg. She deserved extra rations.

Mum took a deep breath. "Do you two girls know anything about this... this... travesty of normality?"

I looked at my feet, and Willow squeezed her thumb between the fingers of her other hand.

"I'll take that as a yes then," glowered Mum.

Willow began to speak. "It was an accident — "

"I want to hear it from my mother's mouth," said Mum, regaining her composure, and beginning the walk over the lawn towards the partying couple.

Granny looked up and spat liquid from her mouth. She fumbled with the radio, and the music stopped. A lone crow squawked in a nearby tree, and the chickens seemed to move forward a fraction.

"Don't speak, Boris," hissed Granny, in a voice

that everybody in the garden heard. "Act dumb! I've got this."

Boris blew smoke from his nostrils and stared in terror at the approaching behemoth that was my angry mother. He coughed and spluttered and looked up at Mum as she came to a halt directly before him. "Maaaa? Baaaa?" he said.

Mum studied the goat for a second or two before turning her gaze on Granny, who sucked at her straw and smiled. "Good morning, dear. Fancy a cocktail?"

With her hands on her hips, Mum bent at the waist and looked Granny directly in the eyes. "It's not even midday, Mother. Now, I'm giving you two choices. You either tell me exactly what's going on here, or I go straight to the haven and tell everybody who respects you that you're drinking alcohol before noon with a goat which you've quite obviously enchanted."

Granny sighed. "The game's up, Boris. It was good while it lasted. Take Penny and Willow indoors and show them your study. I'll talk to Maggie."

"Study?" spluttered Mum. "Your goat's got a study!"

Boris got to his feet and cleared his throat. "Allow me to introduce myself, dear lady. I'm — "

Mum's scowl scared even the chickens, and Boris took a stumbling step backwards. "I'll show the young ladies my study," he said in a low voice, with his head bowed.

Willow and I followed Boris across the lawn and picked up the Tupperware boxes. Mum waited until we'd opened the back door to the cottage before unloading her verbal barrage on Granny.

"Is that my father's fly tying vice with a cigar in it?" shouted Mum.

"Boris likes to smoke," said Granny. "We tried taping a cigar to his hoof, but it didn't work out so well. He fell asleep after a few drinks with the cigar still lit. It's a good job the fire brigade gave out those free smoke alarms or Boris would have had more than a few singed hairs."

Boris held up his leg and showed us the browned hairs above his hoof.

"I am about to explode!" yelled Mum.

Boris shook his head. "Poor, poor Gladys," he said. "All she's tried to do is be good to me."

I laughed. "Don't worry about her," I said. "She'll twist Mum around her little finger within ten minutes." If Granny remembered to tell Mum she'd been helping us with our magic, as Willow had suggested when we'd blackmailed her for the spell book, she'd calm Mum down within five minutes. I smiled at Boris. "Come on, let's see this study of yours."

Boris led us through the cottage, and pushed open the door to Granny's back room with his nose. Willow looked at me, and I raised my eyebrows. Neither of us had been in the back room for months, and as far as we knew, neither had anyone else.

Granny's back room overlooked the rear garden, and was her home's showpiece. It was the room reserved for revered guests, or people she wanted to impress. It was an important person who was invited into the back room of Granny's cottage. It was an exceptionally lucky individual who was granted permission to convert Granny's back room into a study — especially a study that was a cross between a barn and the office of a nineteen seventies TV private eye.

An ashtray filled with cigar butts, placed next to the laptop computer on a low coffee table, masked the usual scent of expensive beeswax and furniture polish, and most of the deep pile carpet was embedded with white goat hair. A dog cushion with a goat shaped dip in it was placed in front of the table, and drinking glasses with straws in them dotted every available surface, some with an inch of amber liquid still in the base.

Willow picked one up and held it up to the light. "This is Granny's best cut crystal," she said.

"You don't put good brandy in cheap glasses, Willow," Boris said, curling up on the cushion in front of the table. "It ruins the experience. Come here, let me show you my blog."

Boris spoke into the microphone next to the

computer. "Wake up," he commanded. The computer flashed to life, and a smiling picture of Boris greeted us on the screen. "Granny took the photo," he said. "She really caught my good side. That's the picture I'm using for my blog!"

"You've got to be kidding!' I said. "You can't write a blog as a goat, Boris!"

"Don't worry, Penelope," said Boris. "I shall be pretending I'm a human writing as a goat. There's all sorts of things on the internet these days. People will be none the wiser. They'll think I'm a mad man."

Laughter from the garden caught my attention, and I looked through the window to see Mum and Granny walking towards the cottage, both of them smiling. "Told you, Boris," I said. "Granny's calmed Mum down already."

Mum walked into the study ahead of Granny and stared at the mess. She smiled at Boris, ignoring the chaos. "I'm Maggie. It's nice to meet you, Boris"

Boris stood up and bowed his head. "I'm pleased to make your acquaintance," he said. "Gladys has told me a lot about you."

Granny stepped forward and winked at me. "I've told your mother how I've been helping you girls with your magic," she said. "I've always felt it was my duty to aid you both in furthering your skills, and as your grandmother and mentor, I'm very proud of you both. Giving you that book that meant so much to me, and showing you how to use it, was more than just an extremely generous gesture on my behalf, it was my way of letting you both know how much I love you."

Granny was really over egging the pudding, but Mum was lapping it up. "You've done a wonderful job," she said, touching Granny's arm. "Penelope even detected one of Eva's spells in a blueberry muffin this morning." She gazed at me and Willow adoringly. "These girls will get into the haven sooner than I ever expected if they carry on the way they are."

'How wonderful," said Boris. "It's lovely to see a family so close. It could bring a goat to tears."

I rolled my eyes at Willow, and she giggled.

"Boris," said Mum. "Would you mind if Gladys took me upstairs and showed me Charleston?"

"Not at all," said Boris, "but you must promise not to try and reverse Gladys's spell. I'm quite happy as I am. Happier than I've ever been in fact."

Mum crouched in front of Boris. "I promise," she said, holding the back of her hand an inch from Boris's nostrils.

"He's not a dog, Mum," I said. "He doesn't need to smell your hand!"

"I thought it would gain his trust," said Mum. "I'm sorry if I offended you, Boris. It's going to take some time to get used to you."

"No apology required," said Boris. "I'm perfectly aware of how strange this situation is."

My phone buzzed in my pocket. It was a text from Susie.

The results from toxicology have come back. The police said it isn't drugs in Sam's stomach. It's oriental pine pollen.

I showed Willow the text, and her eyes widened. She'd come to the same conclusion as me.

I sent Susie a reply.

Meet us at the nursing home.

"Mum," I said. "Can I borrow your car?"

"Take mine, girls," said Granny. "I can't drive today. I don't know how many mojitos I've had, but I feel quite giddy. Are you going anywhere nice?"

"To see a woman about a potion," I said.

CHAPTER TWENTY

"You don't think the potion had anything to do with Sam's death do you?" asked Willow as we climbed the steps to the nursing home entrance.

"Of course not," Susie said, "that's why I didn't say anything to the police. They think the pollen's from a food supplement. I thought we'd give Veronica a chance to explain why she'd given Sam a libido boosting potion before the police get involved. The least we can do is prepare her for any embarrassment coming her way."

I laughed. "Veronica and Sam? I doubt it. If you believe Jason Danvers, Sam was into men these days anyway."

"He was married to a woman," said Susie. "He obviously liked both sexes."

"Veronica's old enough to be his mother," I said, opening the door and stepping inside the home. "And she's with Ron. I very much doubt that potion was in Sam's stomach to help his little guardsman stand to attention."

The three of us laughed as we approached the reception desk, but straightened our faces as an angry man stormed from a corridor to our right. "I don't know why I pay so much to live here," he shouted, "if you can't even replace gym equipment when it goes missing!"

"We've ordered a whole new set of weights, Mr Richards," said the petite nurse rushing after him. "It's only one little bar that's been misplaced. There's plenty of other equipment you can use."

"I need both dumbbells," protested the man. "Or I'll have one arm bigger than the other."

"Can't you do one arm at a time?" asked the flustered nurse.

The man turned on the spot. "I pay more money a month to live here than you *earn* in a month, young lady. I shouldn't have to put up with this nonsense. Just make sure those weights get delivered soon!"

The nurse sighed as Mr Richards stomped off, his lycra clad belly bouncing as he flounced around the corner. "I'm sorry you had to witness that," she said. "Mr Richards has got a short fuse. How can I help you?"

"We're here to visit Veronica Potter," I said.

She smiled. "Oh good, the poor woman needs cheering up."

"Is she okay?" asked Willow.

The nurse winked. "Man trouble," she giggled. "Do you three know Veronica well?"

"Well enough," I smiled.

"So you know about her relationship with Ronald?"

Willow nodded. "Oh yes, we know *all* about that."

"It seems they're having a few problems," said the nurse. "They've been arguing a lot and Veronica's quite upset. She's probably in her room, go on through, she'll be happy to see you." She walked back the way she'd come, muttering to herself about selfish old rich people.

Willow, susie, and I made our way through the lounge and along the corridor which led to Veronica's room. Her door was closed, and the sound of loud sobbing came from the other side. Willow knocked, and Veronica stopped crying and cleared her throat. "Come in!" she called.

Willow opened the door and the three of us entered together. Veronica was on her bed with an open book on her chest and scrunched up tissues surrounding her. Her face was devoid of make-up and she looked twenty years older. "Oh, it's you three," she said. "I thought it might be nurse with a sedative."

"Are you alright, Veronica?" I said, sitting on the bed and taking her trembling hand in mine. "What's happened?"

"Oh, Penelope," she said. "It was awful. Ron lost his temper because I went for a walk around the grounds with Wally. Wally picked a flower and Ron saw him giving it to me. He called me terrible names and said I was a cheat."

Willow sat on the other side of the bed, and Susie perched near Veronica's feet.

"That's horrible," said Willow. "I hope you gave as good as you got."

"I tried," sobbed Veronica, "but he teased me about my make-up. He said I looked like a painted sex clown!" She took a fresh tissue from the box beside her and blew her nose. "It's over now. I'm a free woman again." She managed a small smile. "Don't you girls worry about me. It won't take me long to find a new breakfast companion. I'll soon bounce back with lovely young ladies like you visiting me."

"What a nasty man," I said. "I've got a good mind to go and tell him what I think of him."

Veronica squeezed my hand. "He's in no mood for visitors, dear. He's hardly left his room in a week. As far as I'm concerned he can rot in there!" Veronica released my hand and dragged herself into a seated position. "Enough about my woes," she said. "You know what they say, misery loves company."

I smiled at her. "That's exactly what they say."

Veronica managed another smile. "So, girls, to what do I owe the pleasure of this visit? No one knew about mine and Ron's problems outside of the home, so you didn't come here to console me."

I glanced at Susie and Willow. Susie looked away, and Willow gave me a gentle nod of encouragement.

"It's a sensitive matter, Veronica," I said. "It's about that potion I made for you."

Veronica's face whitened. "What about it?" she said, clutching a tissue to her chin.

"Is it possible that Sam Hedgewick could have drank any of it, Veronica?" I asked with care.

Veronica's body shook, and she broke into gasping sobs that rocked the bed. "I knew it would come back to haunt me," she wailed. "I don't know why I thought I could get away with it! I should have told the police when I had the chance. They were sure to find out with all their fancy modern equipment. It's not like in the old days! I don't know why I thought I'd get away with it! I'm in a lot of trouble, aren't I?"

Willow stared at Veronica slack jawed, and Susie sat upright.

"What are you saying, Veronica?" I said. "Did you hurt Sam?"

Veronica gasped. "No! Of course not, but I'm

guilty as charged of administering a substance to an unwitting recipient! I only wanted to stop him driving under the influence of alcohol! Are the police coming for me? Will I go to jail? I don't think I could take jail. Your grandmother only spent three hours in a police cell, and it broke her, Penelope."

I rolled my eyes at Willow. The only thing broken by Granny's stay in a cell was the police station kettle, and the teabag fund.

Veronica sighed as I helped her sit fully upright and plumped up her pillow. "Tell us what happened," I said.

"It was during the argument I had with Sam," said Veronica, "about him driving under the influence."

I nodded my encouragement. "Go on, what happened?"

"Earlier in the night I'd given Ron some of the potion, you know, to try and get a little warm blood in his veins, but it didn't work." Veronica paused and gazed at her feet. "Well, that's not entirely true. The part of the potion that you made to help Ron sleep worked just fine — he went out like a light. He snored like a pig too."

"Why did you give Sam some of it?" asked Susie.

"I didn't want him to drive! He'd had far too many beers, and not that horrible stuff from Belgium. He was drinking that strong local beer from Wickford brewery. You know, the one with the picture of the rock music guitar player on the tin?"

"Wickford headbanger," said Willow. "That is strong stuff."

"He'd had one and a half!" said Veronica. "I'm sure he'd have struggled to open his car door, let alone drive the thing."

Susie coughed. "That *is* a lot," she said tactfully.

It was too much to consider driving after, but nowhere near the amount Susie and I had drank on a regular basis when we'd been teenagers — usually behind the youth club, but often in my grandfather's potting shed. Granny had caught us once and threatened to tell Mum, but had soon calmed down when she'd tasted the beer and pulled up an old crate to sit on and join us. Granny had managed to drink three before finally succumbing and falling asleep with her head on an open bag of compost.

Veronica took a deep breath. "I'm glad you agree," she said. "I thought maybe I'd overreacted. I just didn't want Sam hurting himself or somebody else, so I poured the rest of the potion into his beer, hoping it would make him fall asleep. There are plenty of spare rooms here, he could have stayed the night." Veronica shook her head. "It didn't work though, he didn't get sleepy, and eventually he agreed to take a taxi home. He couldn't get one of course, so he walked home, and you three know how that worked out for him."

Veronica broke into sobs again. "It feels so good to finally get that off my chest! I know I didn't kill Sam, but I do wonder whether he'd have been able to fight off his attacker if I hadn't slipped that potion in his drink."

"He was attacked from behind," Susie said. "I doubt he even heard his attacker coming. There were no signs of a struggle, Veronica. You weren't to blame in any way at all."

"I heard on the news that they'd caught a man," said Veronica. "I hope they lock him in and throw the key at a book!"

There were far too many things wrong with Veronica's sentence, so we all let it go.

"We'll see," I said. "The police are still investigating."

"The man on the radio said the killer was hiding at the car show," Veronica said. "The organisers said the police ruined the last day, running around and looking in everybody's tents and cars!"

"In all fairness to the police, they were looking for a murderer," said Willow.

"The whole things shocking," continued Veronica. "And to think the suspect was a soldier too! He's brought shame on Her Majesty's Armed Forces. That's what he's done!"

Susie looked blank. "The police didn't tell me that

at the press conference," she said. "Who told you that, Veronica?"

Veronica dabbed the last of the tears from beneath her eyes. "The man on the radio. He said they were trying to find out if the suspect was connected with the RAC. He was wearing a badge on his clothing apparently. You girls really should pay attention."

"We know that, Veronica," said Willow. "That's the reason the police thought he was at the car show. Most of those vintage car owners are members of the Royal Automobile Club. The suspect owns a few old cars himself. Nobody said he was a soldier though."

Veronica gave a sigh of relief. "That's good to know. I hate the armed forces being brought into disrepute. I thought the radio presenter had meant the Royal Armoured Corps. Ron would have been livid to know one of his own was the killer!"

CHAPTER TWENTY-ONE

"Veronica," I said. "Has Ron ever been violent?"

Willow and Susie fidgeted, casting me nervous glances. We'd all come to the same conclusion, and the atmosphere in the room had electrified.

Veronica furrowed her brow and narrowed her eyes. "That's an odd question, Penelope," she said. "I may be old, and I know I get my proverbs muddled up from time to time, but stupid I am not. I saw all your faces drop when I mentioned the Royal Armoured Corps." Veronica looked at each of us, her cheeks reddening. "You think Ron killed Sam! Admit it!"

I stood up just in time to avoid being hit by Veronica's legs as she swung them off the bed and stood up. She pointed at the door. "Go!" she said.

"You're throwing us out?" said Willow. "Veronica, just think things through for a moment. Is there any chance at all that Ron could have — "

"I'm not throwing you out," said Veronica, marching towards the door. "I'm coming with you to confront that old sod! I think there's every chance he killed Sam. So many things are making sense now."

"Like what?" I said.

"I'm saving those questions for Ronald! Let me at him!"

Susie beat Veronica to the door and put her back against it. "Calm down for a moment, Veronica," she said. She took her phone from her bag. "We need to phone the police first."

"Wait," I said, as Susie dialled. "Let me ring Barney on his personal phone. We don't want cars full of police turning up here and scaring all the residents, and I'd like Barney to be the one who makes the arrest if it was Ron who killed Sam. He deserves it."

Veronica reached past Susie and grabbed the door handle. "You telephone Barney, Penelope, but we're going to get the confession from Ron before he gets here. Ron will clam up in front of authority, the army did that to him, but I'll get what you want to know out of him! Oh, I'll get it out of him all right!"

I dialled Barney as Veronica pulled the door open with an angry tug, making Susie stumble. Barney answered the phone, and I spoke quickly as I followed Veronica along the corridor towards Ron's room, with Willow and Susie on either side of me. "Come to the nursing home," I said. "Quickly. I'll explain when you get here. We'll be in Ron's room. I'm not sure what number it is."

"Fifty-three," snapped Veronica, glancing over her shoulder.

"Room fifty-three," I repeated. "Hurry, Barney."

I slipped the phone into my pocket and took a deep breath. I was about to see somebody being accused of murder, and I was more nervous than the first time I'd kissed a boy. Muscles cramped in my stomach, and my legs struggled to hold my weight.

Veronica stopped outside Ron's door, and I looked at Willow for support. Her face was white and her bottom lip was crushed between her teeth. It was a relief to know I wasn't the only person who was terrified.

Veronica showed no such nervous tendencies. She paused for the briefest of moments, sucked a lungful of air into her chest, muttered something under her breath, and swung the door open with a shove so violent a painting in the hallway shifted on its mounting.

"What have you done?" she screamed as she entered the room with the rest of us close behind her. "What did you do?"

Ron stared at us from his seat. A few days worth

of grey stubble cloaked his chin and cheeks, and I had to remind myself that the person I was looking at was a potential murderer, not simply an elderly man in his dressing gown and slippers. A well built elderly man, but elderly nonetheless. "What are you babbling on about, Veronica?" he spat. "If you've got a problem with me, come here on your own, not with your little army of troublemakers."

I hadn't been labeled a troublemaker since I'd left the school gates behind me for the last time, six years ago. Veronica didn't appreciate the insult either. "How dare you speak about them in that way!" she shouted. "They're here so I don't have to confront a monster like you on my own!"

Ron scratched his chin with long fingernails. "You've lost your marbles, Veronica," he scoffed. "What the heck are you talking about, woman?"

Veronica approached him and bent at the waist, placing her face inches from his. "I'm talking about you killing Sam Hedgewick. I don't know why you did it, or how you did it, but my gut says you did it, and this gut hasn't been wrong for three decades."

"Get lost," said Ron. "Get out of my room and go and find Wally. You've been flirting with him for weeks woman, you're a common wh — "

"I was wrong," said Veronica, in a tone so menacing my eye twitched. "My gut *has* been wrong in the last three decades. It was wrong on the day I said yes to your invitation to watch you play in the Wickford bowls championship final. I *should* have gone with Wally when he asked me. I doubt he needs a special potion to get his compass pointing north. He certainly knew how to handle those big balls of his, and he beat you at bowls that day, didn't he, Ron?"

Ron's smirk tightened into a scowl, and a flash of anger darkened his eyes. "Shut up, Veronica, or — "

Veronica tilted her head and moved her face even closer to Ron's, her nose almost touching his. "Or what, Ronald? You'll kill me like you did Sam?"

Ron's hands tightened into fists, and I took a step forward, sucking air into my mouth and tasting copper. I wasn't sure what spell I was about to cast, but it felt right. I pressed my fingers together, but just as I was about to click them, Ron relaxed his hands and laughed. "This is silly," he said, leaning back in his seat. "Come on, Veronica. We had a good time together, but it's over. There's no need to come here making crazy accusations."

I blew out air and flexed my hand. It had been close, and electricity still tingled in my fingertips.

"Answer some questions for me, Ron," said Veronica. "If you didn't kill Sam you'll have all the answers, won't you?"

Ron crossed his arms and smiled. "Ask away," he said.

Veronica straightened her body and stared down at

Ron. "Why was your door locked on the night of the party? The night Sam was killed. I came here two or three times, but you didn't answer when I knocked."

"Because you gave me some of that bloody potion, you daft old bag. It knocked me right out, didn't it? Probably so you could have fun at the party without me."

Veronica pointed at Ron's hand. "How did you get that injury, Ron? It doesn't look like a strain from weight lifting. It looks bruised."

"I dropped a heavy bar on it," said Ron. "Next question." He looked at me, Willow, and Susie. "Enjoying the show, girls? Do you like watching a mad woman bullying an old man?"

"It's best you just answer her questions, Ron," I said.

"And to think I gave you all those green beans last year," he growled. "You can forget about any next year, and I'll make sure everyone else at the allotment knows how cruel you are. There'll be no more free vegetables for you, Penelope."

Veronica laughed. "We don't even know if the allotments will even be there next year, you old fool. The land owner's dead. Remember? You won't be growing beans next year anyway, Ron. You'll be behind bars, where you belong."

"Have you finished, woman?" said Ron. "I want you out of this room, and out of my life."

'I've got one more question for you, Ronald."

Ron waved a hand. "Hurry then, I haven't got all day."

Veronica pointed at the wardrobe built into the wall behind Ron's seat. "What are you hiding in there?" she breathed.

Ron's whole body tensed. His striped pyjamas tightened across his chest, and the tendons in his neck bulged. "I'm not hiding anything. Now get out. I've answered your questions."

"What's in there, Ron?" pressed Veronica. "You haven't let me put your clean washing away all week, and you've moved your seat so you can sit there guarding the wardrobe."

"I moved my seat here because I fancied a change. That's all."

"You can't even see your television from there, Ron," said Veronica. "Do you think I'm stupid?"

'Why don't you just let Veronica have a look, Ron?" said Willow. "The police are on their way. You'll be forced to open it when they get here."

Ron's whole demeanour changed. "Oh, the police are coming are they? Why didn't you say that in the first place?"

He stood up, towering over Veronica. He pushed out his chest, rolled his shoulders, and rocked his head from side to side, stretching his neck muscles. Veronica stepped backwards as Ron grabbed the seat and pulled it away from the wardrobe. He slid the door open and bent over, fumbling around in the bottom. Veronica moved forward and tried to look over Ron's shoulder. "What are you doing?" she said. "What have you got in there, Ron?"

Ron's voice echoed in the wardrobe. "You'd better phone the police," he said, "and tell them to bring an ambulance with them."

For such a large and elderly man, Ron moved quickly. He stood up, span on the spot, and raised a hand above his head. A glint of silver caught my eye, and Veronica shrieked. "No, Ron!"

Ron swung the metal bar in an arc towards Veronica's head, and either Susie or Willow screamed behind me. Copper flooded my mouth and filled my throat, and my fingers stung with the force of the electricity which coursed through them. A sizzle accompanied the click of my fingers, and the metal bar stopped moving, centimetres from Veronica's frightened face.

"Catch her!" I shouted, as Veronica's legs shook and gave way beneath her.

Willow leapt forward and caught Veronica as she fainted. Susie helped carry her to the bed, and Ron stared at me with wide frightened eyes. "What's happening," he said. "I can't move."

"Never mind what's happening," I said. I nodded at the metal bar in Ron's hand. It was red with dried blood, and a few hairs stuck to it. "I take it that's the murder weapon? The missing weights bar from the gym."

Ron nodded, his eyes dropping to the purple sparks which arced between my finger tips as I held my hand at waist height. Interesting, I thought. He could communicate and move his eyes, but the rest of his body was completely paralysed. I wasn't sure what spell I'd cast, or how I'd learnt it. I didn't remember reading a spell like it in Granny's book, but maybe my subconscious brain had stored it in my mind as I'd been flicking through the pages. I'd have to ask Granny.

"What are you?" stammered Ron.

"What do you think I am, Ron?" I said. "I'm a witch of course, and if you don't tell me exactly what you did to Sam, and why you did it, you won't be going to jail, you'll be swimming around in that pond outside, croaking and eating flies."

Ron grimaced. "Okay, I'll tell you!"

I raised my hand and turned it in the air, sparks sizzling and crackling from my fingers. "Talk."

"I was jealous. I've always been a jealous man. It's my flaw."

"Jealous of Sam?"

Ron nodded.

"Why?"

"That potion you made for Veronica. It didn't

work the way she wanted on me, it only made me drowsy. I missed the party because I was asleep, and when I woke up I was hungry so I went to see if there was any food left, and then I saw it!"

"Saw what?" I said.

"Veronica spiking Sam's drink with the passion potion! She couldn't get what she wanted from me, so she found the next available man to try it out on! It didn't work on Sam either though, so when he left, I followed him. I'd lost my temper, I didn't know what I was doing! I just wanted to warn him to stay away from Veronica, but I hit him too hard."

"You're a vile pig, Ron. You got out through the door with the broken alarm, didn't you? So nobody knew you had left. You locked your door so people would think you were asleep." said Veronica. She'd woken up.

I turned to her. "I can explain," I said, looking at my sparking hand.

"There's no need, dear." she said. "You can tell me in your own time. Concentrate on getting the rest of the confession out of him. Your police friend will be here soon, and I'm not sure you want him to see you in such a compromising situation."

She was right. I'd had it drilled into me since I was old enough to speak that I should do everything I could to prevent mortals from discovering the existence of witches. In the past week alone I'd cast a spell on a lawyer, a boat owner, and now a murderer. A talking goat had attacked an intruder on my boat, and I was in the process of performing magic in front of one of the biggest gossips in town. I wasn't doing too well at the whole keeping witchcraft a secret thing, and I didn't want to add Barney to the growing list of witnesses to my magic.

Ron grunted. "It hurts," he said. "All my muscles ache."

"Think how much pain Sam felt," spat Veronica. She stood up, pushed passed Ron, and bent down to rummage in his wardrobe. She held a black piece of clothing aloft. "Exhibit B!" she said.

She turned the blazer around and showed us all the badge. The owner of the *Flirting Kingfisher* had been correct. There was a crown, and the letters RAC were below it. We'd all been too quick to assume the badge the boat owner had recalled while under my spell was the same as the badge on the front of the car next to the canal.

"I don't understand," said Willow. "Why did you bring the murder weapon and the blazer back here, Ron? There's probably evidence on the blazer, and there's *definitely* evidence on the weights bar. Why didn't you throw them in the canal?"

"He wouldn't throw his blazer away," said Veronica. "It meant too much to him."

"It's been wth me for forty years," said Ron. "Of

course I wouldn't toss it in the canal. I was going to return the bar to the gym, but I panicked. I thought I'd keep it hidden until all the fuss died down."

"You call a murder investigation *fuss*," said Veronica. "You really are a piece of work, aren't you?"

Ron swivelled his eyes, attempting to look at Veronica. "I did it because I loved you, Veronica. I couldn't bear it when I saw you giving Sam that potion. The thought of his hands all over you, and the fact that you wanted him to do it sent me mad!"

"I put that potion in his drink to try and make him fall asleep," said Veronica. "So he wouldn't drive home after drinking. You're a fool, Ronald. A murdering, sadistic, jealous fool, and I hope you get what you deserve!"

Footsteps sounded in the hallway outside. "It's that room on the right, officer Dobkins," said a woman's voice.

"Quick," said Veronica. "Stop doing whatever it is you're doing, Penelope!"

My fingers stopped tingling and the spell broke. Ron's arm continued the swinging arc through the air to my front, and Barney roared a warning as he entered the room. "Drop the weapon," he shouted. "Get out of the way, Penelope!"

I moved aside as Barney ran at Ron, his nightstick above his head and anger on his face. "How dare you attack Penny," he shouted, twisting Ron's arm behind his back. The metal bar thudded on the carpet, and Barney kicked it away. "If I wasn't in uniform, I'd do more than put handcuffs on you, you piece of — "

I touched Barney's arm. "He wasn't attacking me — "

"Yes he was," said Veronica, raising her eyebrows at me. "And he killed Sam Hedgewick. That's the murder weapon on the floor. I think you'll find it matches Sam's wound perfectly. Well done, constable! You've bagged yourself a killer!"

Ron groaned. "That girl's a witch," he said, looking at me.

Veronica bristled. "And you're a bast — "

"Everybody, calm down!" demanded Barney. "Will somebody please tell me what's going on here?"

CHAPTER TWENTY-TWO

*D*aisies had started showing their heads again, and the grass around my mooring was an inch too long. Barney wiped a hand over his sweaty brow as he pushed the lawn mower. "Would you like another drink? I yelled, making myself heard over the petrol engine.

Barney shook his head, his face red, and his ginger fringe stuck to his damp forehead. His white torso glared in the sun, and the two layers of sun cream had begun running down his chest. "No thanks," he shouted, forcing the mower over a bump in the ground. "I haven't got much left to do, and then I have to go to the police station before I go home and get ready for the party."

Willow poured me another iced water from the

jug on the picnic bench. "Isn't it exciting?" she said. "You and me living together on a boat!"

"We should raise the rent," said Tony from beside me. "You'll be using more electricity now."

Michelle slapped his hand. "He's joking, girls!'

I wasn't so sure.

Mabel snarled at Tony, and he shooed her away with the hem of his striped apron. Although Tony and Michelle employed two full time chefs, Tony still insisted on working in the hotel kitchen. He'd made a deal with Michelle — when either of the chefs could make a Lancashire hotpot as legendary as his, he'd put his kitchen duties behind him and help Michelle run the rest of the hotel. I doubted it would happen soon. I'd never tasted a Lancashire hotpot like Tony's, even in Lancashire.

"You need to keep that goose under control," said Tony. "It scared all the customers in the beer garden last night, and ate half a chicken from a plate." He looked around the clearing. "She stole the basket too. It's probably around here somewhere."

"We were having a seventies themed food night," explained Michelle. She tapped her husband's hand again. "Anyway, Tony. It's not their goose. It just happens to live here."

"Are you sure you two won't come down for a drink later?" I asked, guiding the subject away from enchanted animals.

"We can't, dear," said Michelle, the scent of her expensive perfume competing with the aroma of freshly mowed grass. "The hotel's too busy to step away from for even a minute in the evening, but you two enjoy your party — it must be so exciting for you both. Two sisters living together on a boat."

It was exciting, and it was surprisingly all thanks to Mum. She'd been the person responsible for suggesting the idea to Willow, and I'd jumped at the chance of having my sister living and working with me. We'd already planned a two week trip along the canals, and were leaving the next day. The school summer holidays were starting in two days time, and the touristy villages and towns along the waterways would be brimming with holidaymakers and potential customers.

"It's hardly a party," I said. "It's just a small gathering of family and friends."

"That's the best kind of party," said Michelle with a smile. She gave Tony a playful dig in his ribs. "Come on, big boy," she said. "The hotel won't book the guests in itself."

The couple made their way back up the hill to the hotel, ignoring Mable who ran in circles around their feet. Rosie leapt up onto the picnic bench, and rubbed herself on my bare arm, ignoring the goose when it came bolting back towards us. Mabel jumped up at the picnic bench, barking and growling at Rosie, who padded to the edge of the tabletop. She watched Mabel intently as she bounced up and down, and when the time was right, landed a perfectly timed paw swipe on her beak.

The goose let out a whelp of shock, and sat down, gazing up at Rosie, averting her eyes when Rosie stared back.

"There," I said, stroking Rosie's back. "I knew you could be friends. It only took Boris to prove to you that Mabel isn't so dangerous."

"I don't think they're friends exactly," said Willow. "I just think the tables have turned. Rosie's the boss now."

Mabel lay submissively on her back and presented Rosie with her fat belly and extended neck. The cat leapt down from the table and sniffed at the bird's white feathers, before turning her back and sauntering away, leaping onto the boat and disappearing inside.

The mowers engine spluttered and stopped, and the birds began singing again. "Finished," shouted Barney.

He'd done a good job, and I grabbed his t-shirt from the table and walked it over to him. "Bend down," I said, as I stood in front of him.

Barney smiled and lowered his head, his lips puckered as he leaned towards my face.

"What are you doing?" I said, guiding his t-shirt over his head.

Barney's face turned a deep shade of crimson. "I'm sorry," he mumbled. "I thought you were going to give me a thank you kiss. Not a full kiss of course. Just a peck on the lips." The hue in his cheeks spread to his neck. "Or the cheek."

"Your hands are dirty, Barney," I said, "you'd have got fingerprints all over your white t-shirt. I was just trying to help."

Barney stood up straight again. "Thank you," he said, his face still matching the colour of my shorts.

He pushed the lawnmower towards the path. "I'll just take this back to my dad. He want's to do his own lawn tomorrow. Then I've got to go to the station and finish the paperwork for Jason Danvers's bail conditions. He's being released from custody today."

It had been six days since Ron had been arrested and charged with the murder of Sam Hedgewick. I'd convinced the police not to charge Jason with breaking into my boat, even threatening Sergeant Cooper with the promise that I'd stand up in court and say I'd invited him aboard if I had too. Barney had told me that without the additional charge of breaking and entering, it was likely that Jason would be awarded a suspended sentence for the crime he was already wanted for. The thought of him having lost Sam, and then having to languish in jail, had been too much for me, and I'd dropped the charges happily.

I caught up to Barney and tapped him on the back.

"Bend down," I said, as he turned around. His constant blushing was becoming a little too much, and I smiled as I gave him a kiss on his reddened warm cheek.

He stood up straight with a wide grin on his face, and his whistling echoed through the trees as he pushed the mower up the footpath, almost tripping over his own feet once or twice.

I sat down opposite Willow on the bench, and we opened the bottle of elderberry wine that was waiting for us in the shade beneath the table. The clink of our glasses startled Mabel, and we kept our drinks touching as I made a toast. "Here's to life together on the water," I said.

Granny and Boris arrived first. Boris had wanted to be one of the first at the party so he could speak freely for a while before the rest of the guests arrived. "Here they are!" said Granny, as she placed her backpack on the table and hugged us both in turn. "My special little homicide detectives!"

Willow laughed, freeing herself from Granny's arms. "We didn't solve the crime," she said. "It was a joint effort. Veronica actually came up with the most important clue, and Penny's magic extracted the full confession."

"Well, we're extremely proud of you both, and Susie of course, aren't we Boris?"

"Profoundly," said Boris, inspecting his hooves. "Although I can't help observing that my part in all of this has been played down a little. If you remember, it was I who discovered and proceeded to entrap the man we wrongly assumed to be the villain. Of course, at the time, I had no idea he was innocent. I placed my life in the direst of danger, and not a mention of my heroism has been made in the newspaper."

"Not this again, Boris," said Granny. "Will you stop harping on about it if I pour you a drink?"

Boris lifted his head. "Naturally."

"Boris can't drink alcohol!" I said. "Barney will be here soon, and Veronica and Wally are coming. How do we explain why a goat is drinking Brandy?"

"Veronica knows you're a witch now, Penny, although I suspect she's known about our family since her and I were teenagers."

"She doesn't know Boris is a man in a goat's body," I protested, 'but go on, what happened when you are a teenager?"

"It was a cold winter," said Granny, pushing her glasses along the bridge of her nose and sitting down next to Willow. "Wages were low and tensions were running high in the town. You have to remember that back then we didn't have computer games, we had to make our own fun, and fun was hard to come by. There was no — "

Boris snorted. "Cut to the chase, Gladys. I need that drink."

Granny fixed Boris with a fiery stare, but Boris simply nudged the backpack with his nose.

"I turned Veronica's uncle into a garden gnome," said Granny. "A gnome with a fishing rod — Harold enjoyed casting a fly."

"You turned Veronica's uncle into a garden gnome and you *suspect* she knew our family were witches?" I said. "How did you turn him into a garden gnome when you were that age anyway? That's powerful magic!"

"I practiced a lot, dear. Like I said, it was a cold winter and wages were low — "

"You turned a man into a garden gnome," said Willow. "Of course Veronica knew you were a witch! And her uncle must have known!"

"I cast a spell of forgetfulness on her," Granny explained, "and on Harold when he transformed back into himself. No damage was done, and they were both fine when they remembered how to walk and talk again, although Veronica's given me odd looks ever since, and Harold began wearing a fez everywhere he went." Granny shrugged. "I may be way wide of the mark of course. Maybe I'm overreacting. It's just a feeling I get about her."

"You're not overreacting," I said. "Good grief, Granny! I'm surprised you haven't been burnt at the stake!"

Boris nudged the backpack again. "Drink."

Granny opened the bag and took out a large glass mixing bowl. She placed it on the grass and withdrew a bottle from the backpack.

"It's mother's ruin," said Boris. "People will think it's water!"

Granny filled the bowl with gin, and Boris began lapping it up. He lifted his head as Mabel approached. "None for you, you're violent enough without alcohol in you."

"Speaking of mother's," said Granny. "Yours is on her way. She's got news for you."

"Mums's coming?" I said. "She said she'd never come anywhere near my boat."

"Boris had a talk with her," explained Granny.

"I once did three years of a five year psychology course," said Boris, "and it's enabled me to get to the source of her difficulties. It transpires that your mother is more afraid of ingesting insects than we imagined. It's not your boat she's snubbing, the boat is simply a convenient excuse. It's the insect life that thrives along the canal banks which keeps her away from you."

"But she doesn't have to eat anything while she's here," I said.

"Phobias have a nasty way of amplifying if left untreated," explained Boris. "In your dear mother's case, it's progressed to a fear of an insect flying into her mouth."

"Poor Mum," said Willow.

Boris licked his lips. "Don't worry. I'm working on it with her. I'm convinced I can cure her, but in the meantime, we've come up with a compromise."

CHAPTER TWENTY-THREE

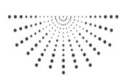

Mum's bee keeper's hat didn't look too out of place. There *were* a lot of insects swarming around the tables laden with food, and we'd told Barney, Veronica, and Wally that Mum was allergic to bites to save her from any embarrassment about her real condition.

Wally was dressed in a tweed jacket with a silk cravat, and spoke about his career as a TV comedy writer as he tucked into sandwiches and cakes. Boris looked on with admiration, and whispered to me as Wally raised another laugh from his captive audience. "I could really get along with that chap," he said.

Nobody mentioned how remarkably quickly Veronica had moved on from Ron, and we thought it best to avoid conversations about the murder altogether.

Susie had shown me the front page of the newspaper when she'd arrived, and as requested, she'd kept mine and Willow's names out of it, but had elevated Barney to hero status. Barney had begrudgingly accepted that we wanted him to take the glory for solving the crime, and had admired the photograph of himself in the newspaper, remarking on how much he resembled Prince Harry.

Willow and I helped Mum onto the boat, and after a few initial reservations about the size and the lack of a full sized freezer, she soon warmed to it, even testing the beds out for comfort and lifting the protective screen on the front of her hat so she could rummage though the stock in my shop.

With a witch on a broomstick fridge magnet in Mum's bag, and another bottle of wine in my hand, we stepped ashore and enjoyed the rest of the evening.

Willow and I sat apart from the group for a while, finishing the bottle of wine and planning our trip. Veronica grabbed an empty glass from the table and joined us, curling her legs beneath herself as she sat on the grass.

"So, you're witches," she said."Just like your grandmother."

Willow looked down. "You know about Granny?" she said, fiddling with her bracelet.

Granny cast nervous glances from her seat and

waved at Veronica, who raised her hand in return. "Of course I do," said Veronica. "She doesn't know it though. She thinks I've forgotten, but I remember what she did that day."

I feigned ignorance. "What day, Veronica? What did she do?"

"It was a long time ago. My uncle had shouted at me and Gladys for throwing stones at the barges on the canal, but we were bored you see, you know how kids can be?"

I nodded.

"Well, he really upset Gladys, and she almost cried. When I saw you at the nursing home with those sparks coming from your fingers, it all came flooding back to me again. That's exactly what Gladys did, but I seem to remember she'd screwed her face up too."

"She does that," said Willow.

"Well, that's when she cast her curse, or whatever you witches call them, and my uncle was never the same again."

'I'm so sorry, Veronica," I said. "For whatever she did."

"No!" Don't be sorry!" laughed Veronica. "I've been wanting to thank Gladys for years, but I didn't know how. I think she thought she was doing something bad to my uncle, but it turned his life around — he was lonely after my aunty died, and thanks to

Gladys, he met the woman he spent the rest of his life with."

"Huh?" spluttered Willow, choking on wine.

Veronica lowered her voice. "She cast a silly curse which made him enjoy wearing ridiculous hats! He took to wearing one of those fez things everywhere he went. When he'd recovered from the plague of course."

"Plague?" I said.

"That was what me and my uncle called it. The doctors had no idea what was wrong with us. We caught it together, and we both forgot how to walk or talk for a month. It was all very odd."

"It sounds awful, but how did wearing a fez change his life?" said Willow, expertly skirting the subject of forgetfulness spells.

"There was a very famous comedian who arrived on the scene, I doubt you've heard of him, Tommy Cooper was his name."

I nodded, but Willow shook her head.

"He was famous for wearing a fez you see, and my uncle loved him! He went to every Tommy Cooper show that he could, and it was at one of his shows that he met Sarah. His life changed from that day forward, and it was all thanks to that lovely woman over there, whispering in her goat's ear."

Veronica sipped her wine. She spat it on the grass

and made a face. "This wine's awful," she said. "Where on earth did you buy it?"

"I made it," I smiled. "It's elderberry."

"Anybody else would apologise and beg your forgiveness," said Veronica. "But not me, I'm honest. Penelope, this wine is vile."

"It is quite awful," said Willow, laughing.

"You'd better get used to it," I smiled, standing up and brushing grass clippings from my legs. "There's twenty-two bottles left on the boat."

As darkness approached, Wally and Veronica left. They walked side by side and linked arms as they reached the steepest part of the hill, disappearing into the gloom together.

Susie broke down into sobs until we reminded her we'd only be gone for two weeks. "We're not going far either" I said, hugging her. "You'll be able to drive out and visit us."

When it was Barney's turn to say goodbye, he lifted and dropped his arms nervously until I took charge of the situation. I wrapped my arms around him and squeezed him tight.

"Thank you for everything you did," he said. "You solved Sam's murder and let me take the credit. I'll never forget. Maybe I could take you out for a meal when you get back — as a thank you of course, nothing else!"

I smiled. "I'd like that, Barney," I said.

Barney turned and waved as he climbed the footpath. "Enjoy your trip!" he shouted.

"Thank goddess they've all gone!" said Mum, when Barney had vanished. "Now we can get down to the real business. I've got some exciting news for you, Penelope."

"I was dying to tell her when I got here!" said Granny, "but I kept my mouth closed! It was so difficult!"

"Thank you. Mother," said Mum. "That was very brave of you."

"Gladys is nothing if not brave," said Boris, staggering to the empty glass bowl and licking the base. "She's a wonderful woman," he mumbled.

"What's the news?" said Willow. "Come on, Mum."

"I went to the haven today," she said, taking a seat at the picnic bench and picking up a mini sausage roll. For a brief moment I thought she was going to eat it, but a moth flew past and she threw the pastry back onto the plate, slapping the crumbs from her hands. "Eva overheard something, Penelope," she continued.

'Tell her!" said Granny, "before I have to!"

"Eva overheard Maeve talking about you, Penelope. She found out what you did in the nursing home, you know, saving Veronica from a metal bar in the head. You remember don't you?"

I sighed. "Yes, Mum, I remember that not insignificant incident in my life from less than a week ago."

"Well Maeve is very impressed, and according to Eva, you can expect your entry spell to be made known to you in the very near future! You'll be able to visit the haven, Penelope! Isn't that exciting!"

"And all thanks to Gladys, because of her willingness to share her spell book with her granddaughters," murmured Boris, before collapsing in a heap. "She's a remarkable woman."

CHAPTER TWENTY-FOUR

Willow pushed the start button and birds flew from the trees as the engine burst into life. We'd intended to leave before eight o'clock in the morning, but it was half past nine as we pushed away from the bank, with Willow in control of the boat, and me instructing her on how to negotiate the boat out of the mooring and onto the canal.

Mabel had gone chasing swans again, and I placed the left over breakfast sausages on the bank for her. Hopefully she'd get back before a lucky water rat found them.

"Wait!" came a man's voice. "Wait!"

Willow looked up. "One of us has got a secret admirer," she said.

The man running down the path moved the huge

bunch of flowers from in front of his face and shouted again.

"It's Jason Danvers," I said. "What on earth does he want?"

I tossed a mooring rope onto the canal bank. "Pull us ashore," I said.

Jason took the rope in one hand, and his muscles bulged as he pulled us the few feet back to shore. He looked far better than the last time I'd seen him, but the last time I'd seen him, he'd been cowering in the corner of my shop with a goat between his legs. It was hardly a fair comparison.

He wore clothes that were obviously expensive, but beyond my limited knowledge of designer wear. Willow would have known what they were, but she was too busy trying to work to how to turn the engine off. "Turn the key," I said. "Just like a car."

Jason pulled us close to the bank and wrapped the rope loosely through the iron hoop in the ground. "I'm glad I made it in time" he panted, still trying to catch his breath. He held the flowers out towards me. "These are for you," he said.

"What are they for?" I asked. Mum had taught me never to take flowers from a man until I knew precisely what his intentions were.

"A thank you," he said, shaking them gently in front of me. "For not sending me to jail. If you hadn't dropped the charges, I'd have been eating stodgy porridge this morning instead of the fried breakfast I just had at the Coffee Pot."

I took the flowers and smelt them. Mum had also taught me that when you finally accepted the flowers, you showed your gratitude. "Thank you," I said. "They're beautiful. You didn't get them from he convenience store though. They're far too nice."

"And they're alive," added Willow.

Jason laughed. "I got them from Emily's florist."

"Emily's is open again?" I said. "I thought Sam had already sold his properties."

Jason's face dropped at the sound of Sam's name, and my throat swelled with guilt. "I'm sorry about Sam," I said. "I didn't really have the time to offer my condolences the last time we met."

Jason smiled. "Thank you," he said. "It's hard, but I can do good things for this town in his name now. I'll keep his memory burning."

"What do you mean?" said Willow, wiping oil from her hand onto the rag that hung from the roof of the boat.

"Sam left all his assets to me. Everything; his money, his properties, his cars. Not that I needed them, I've done well in life for myself."

"Wasn't he getting rid of his properties though?" I said. "Why would he have named you in a will if he was selling everything?" I stopped talking — I realised what I was doing. "Tell me to shut up if I'm being nosy," I added.

"You're not," he said. "You helped the police find out I was innocent, you have every right to know what went on. When he received all those threats and found out his wife was sniffing around his lawyer, he went to a different lawyer in Covenhill and drafted a will with me named as the beneficiary." He paused and tugged at his t-shirt. "He didn't expect to die though, it was just a symbolic dig at his wife and father more than anything else."

"I can understand him wanting to cut his cheating wife out of the will," said Willow, "but why his father?"

"His father was old fashioned," said Jason. "I forced Sam to tell his dad that he was in love with a man. I think it was your grandmother that witnessed the argument I had with him about it? Outside the lawyer's office."

"Yes, that was Granny," Willow said.

'I threatened not to go to Spain with Sam if he didn't tell his father about us. I feel awful, but I just wanted everything to be honest, you know?" Jason dropped his eyes. "Sam had really helped me change in the months I knew him, and the honesty he taught me in my business affairs spilled over into my personal life. I should have let him do it his way."

"Sam's dad didn't take it well, and that's why he cut him out of the will?" I said.

Jason nodded. "He was really horrible to Sam, but I understand why. He's from a different generation. He's suffering now though. He's devastated about the things he said to his son, but I'll make sure he's okay. Financially anyway, I can't help with his conscience."

"Why don't you go to Spain on your own and do the things you planned with Sam?" I said.

"No," he said. "I want to do good things here with Sam's money. I want to help. I've spent most of my life hurting and conning people. I'll spend the rest of my life making amends."

"You've let Emily open the florist's again," I said.

"Along with every other business that Sam was selling," he said. "They've all got their leases back and they're all open again. Which brings me onto the other reason I'm here. I want to do something for you, for helping me, and to make up for the ordeal I put you through on the boat."

"The flowers are enough," I said, bringing them to my nose.

"Hear me out," said Jason. "Your friend Susie did."

I frowned. "Susie?"

"She was on the boat too when that whole... incident occurred. I scared all three of you. I want to make it up to you all."

"What have you done for Susie?" said Willow.

"She's just accepted the keys to a flat above a shop in town," he said. "I overheard her talking to the owner of the Coffee Pot while I was having breakfast, she was telling her the flat she lived in was too big and expensive for her to live alone in after splitting up with..."

"Robert," I filled in.

"Yes, Robert. Anyway, I offered her a flat free of rent for as long as she needs it, and she accepted."

"Free of rent!" said Willow. "I don't blame her!"

"And that's what I want to do for you two," said Jason, smiling.

"We've got a home," Willow said, tapping the roof of the *Water Witch*, "and I've only just moved aboard. I'm not going anywhere."

Jason nodded. "And a beautiful home it is too" he said. "I was quite taken with how cosy it was when I was... stowed away onboard."

"Breaking in," you mean, said Willow. She put her hand to her mouth. "I'm sorry, that was uncalled for, you've been through a lot and you're trying to do the right thing."

"It's okay," said Jason. He looked towards the bow of the boat where the shop was. "I couldn't help noticing how small your shop is, though," he said. "There's barely enough room to swing a cat in there."

"But enough room for a goat to swing a man," I grinned.

Jason winced, and put a hand to his thigh. "The less said about that the better," he said, "but that goat was odd, very odd. The police said it was the pain playing with my mind, but..."

"What about the size of Penny's shop?" said Willow.

The less said about Boris the better.

"That shop I told you about, below the flat Susie's moving into?"

"Yes?" I said.

"I own it now and it's going to be empty within a week, the couple who rent it are retiring. I want you two to have it. I thought maybe you could move your shop there, or start a whole new business, or keep a floating shop and a static shop. It's up to you, and it would be rent free of course."

Willow put her hand on mine. "It's a yes, isn't it, Penny?"

I wasn't sure. Granny had always said nothing in life was free.

"It's right at the top of that path into town," Jason said, pointing up the hill. "Next to that greengrocers with the strange name."

"*The Firkin Gherkin,*" I said. "Mr and Mrs Potter run the shop next door. They're retiring?"

"They said the bottom's fallen out of the VHS rental market. They're quite old aren't they?"

"Bill's expecting a telegram from the Queen on his next birthday," I said. "They didn't just rent videos though. They cut keys too."

"That was the backbone of the business," agreed Willow.

"Well, they've thrown the towel in. They own a villa in Portugal apparently, so they'll need to leave the Queen a forwarding address."

"Come on, Penny," Willow said. "It'll be great! We can live on the boat, and keep the shop on it too. We'll have a shop in town and a shop to take on the canals."

"Can we think about it?" I said.

Jason smiled. "Of course you can. Take as long as you want."

"We'll be back in two weeks. We'll give you an answer then," I said, turning the key in the ignition and pressing the engine start button.

Jason tossed the mooring rope onto the boat, and pushed us away from the bank. "I'll be right here," he said. "I'm buying a house in town. You'll see me around."

Willow took the controls and guided the boat backwards as Jason watched from the bank. She successfully negotiated the corner and put the gearbox into forward gear.

"Hey!" shouted Jason. "That goat did speak didn't it? I have to know!"

My phone buzzed in my pocket. It was a message from an unknown number.

Hey, Penny. This is my new number. Check out my blog. It's live. www.goat2bekidding.com luv Boris.

I smiled. "Of course not!" I shouted at Jason. "Goats can't talk!"

The End

ABOUT THE AUTHOR

Sam Short loves witches, goats, and narrowboats. He really enjoys writing fiction that makes him laugh — in the hope it will make others laugh too!